HUMEIA'S MIND
— AND —
OTHER STORIES

SHARON MCPETERS

authorHOUSE®

AuthorHouse™
1663 Liberty Drive
Bloomington, IN 47403
www.authorhouse.com
Phone: 1 (800) 839-8640

Published by AuthorHouse 08/03/2016

ISBN: 978-1-5246-2066-0 (sc)
ISBN: 978-1-5246-2065-3 (e)

Print information available on the last page.

Any people depicted in stock imagery provided by Thinkstock are models, and such images are being used for illustrative purposes only. Certain stock imagery © Thinkstock.

This book is printed on acid-free paper.

HUMEIA'S MIND

She parked her pink Mercedes in the beach parking lot and went for a swim in the ocean in her velvet fleur de lis bathing suit.

She was lush and voluptuous and brilliant.

The waves broke over her chest.

She loved the ocean.

She swam in the ocean a long time.

The cemetery was as cemeteries always are. She was reading Elizabeth Bowen's <u>Death of the Heart</u> and Rhys and Colette.

Around her all seemed lushness and voluptuousness and sensuousness.

She was lush and artistic.

She had internal richness and lushness.

She was very artistic and very feminine.

She had richness inside.

She liked apricots.

Around her all seemed sensuousness and lushness.

She was a voluptuary.

There weren't any vulgarians in her world.

She was reading Kafka.

It was a Sunday morning. She did not feel that she needed anything.

She realized the worth of some of Kafka's ideas.

She closed the book and went to the beach.

At the beach, she sat on the sand with her woven, straw beach bag plopped next to her.

Her forearms rested on the knees of her raised legs. Her hands dangled in front of her knees like a couple of gangliated spheres.

The ocean is similar to me, she thought. The ocean is Laodicean. It is not the same color as me though. I am beige inside. I was not always beige inside. I am beige inside now though. I have become beige inside because people have hurt me. That is what happens after awhile. Paleness sets in. Beigeness. Now I am just an onlooker, never to be hurt again. I never give. I will never give anything to anyone again. I don't give. I am beige.

Around four o'clock a 4-foot snail approached. He carried a black Samsonite briefcase and wore Nikes.

As it turned out, he was a specialist of preparing premarital agreements.

He left.

Since something has to be done about the everlasting impulse (the feeling of "sex-towardness") marriage is the natural, normal state for human beings, she thought. Society got atleast something right.

She had always been humanity's scapegoat.

She knew herself as the walking residue of humanity's countless cruelties.

When the ocean's wind became stronger, and therefore gave her more sensate pleasure, she walked along the damp sand near the water.

Alone, as always, she looked at the ocean.

She walked along by the water.

She was tired.

She was sad.

She stopped walking.

She continued to rest.

She listened to the ocean.

She walked along by the water again.

She was very sad. She was very hurt.

She sat down on the damp sand near the water.

She cried.

She thought about what she had been reading.

She looked at the ocean.

She went home.

She did not read any more of <u>The Castle</u>.

At home she cried.

Dear No One,

I hurt.

I am crying.

People always abuse me.

Maybe I should be a part of the world of animals instead.

I do not like the human race anymore.

I do not like human beings anymore.

I have not seen a really nice or good person for years.

I will soon be 44 years old.

I think the human race has reached one of those slumps in history. People subsist unenlighteningly and the human heart is snuffed out under tons of mediocrity. The human heart is snuffed out by the passionless hands of the 20th century's idols. The 20th century's idols are uncompassionate mediocrity and purposelessness.

I have given up on the human race.

Nothing great will come of these years of the 20th century.

Each time greatness rears its head, there stand countless reductivists with charts and all sorts of gadgets and instruments, intent, as always, and successful, as always, at beating down and dissecting and classifying the fragile greatness into something understandable, rational and unmysterious.

Greatness finally dies, and in walk the victorious mediocrities, so proud of themselves.

And that's the world I live in.

Thousands of arrogant, mediocre people, living purposeless lives, blind in every way, not even noticing that the greatness of life no longer lives.

So my no one, good bye for today.

Dear No One

I have done enough for this week.

I have been good to people, I have been a good person.

People have not been good to me, though. They have continued on in their mean and petty ways. After awhile, I have to protect myself from them so that they don't destroy me like the woman in Simone De Beauvoir's book.

After awhile, since my goodness is not returned, I have to stop doing nice things for them and protect myself.

I think these types of people can never see anyone except themselves.

That is one thing that is wrong in our world: people do not treasure goodness.

People should treasure and appreciate and value goodness. It is a true virtue.

But they don't. So what happens every time is just that I am a good person and I am good to people and my goodness is kind of wasted, is done for nothing, because people just don't value it and, worse, treat it as an annoyance even, as if goodness gets in the way of their so-called progress. Actually, almost everyone is on the road to nowhere. But they think they're going somewhere but what they really are doing in filling themselves up with false sensations.

After being good to people for days, weeks, months, my entire life, all I get is mistreatment and a "Get out of my way!" as they, as Algren said, "...make their way down the ladder of success."

Dear No One,

Some thoughts can be placed in a box such as the thoughts intruded upon me by afflictive people. The box is closed and the thoughts are no longer healthful for me. Those thoughts, all alike in their nonlife-affirmness, are not in my life anymore. The box is closed. Ungrieved for and with a sense of relief, those thoughts no longer live in me. Such is the way with afflictives.

What does live in me is a sense of great joy, a sense of greatness, the greatness and nobleness, dignity and honorableness inherent in life. I lately read the entire first part of <u>Look Homeward</u>, <u>Angel</u>, by Thomas Wolfe. Last night I read some of <u>Gargantua</u>, by Rabelais.

My freedom is complete. My mind, my spirit, is unintruded upon.

My life has never been fun. I swear, I don't think I know how to have fun. I don't know where to begin to have fun. I'd have to really think about how I can have fun since it is something new to me, something I have never done or had. What would I do for fun? What would I do to have fun? I have never had fun in my life! The movies--did I have fun then and there? What is fun to me?

A hard question--

What is fun to me? How can I have fun?

I have no idea where to begin having fun!

Learn a new piece of music?

Is learning fun to me?

I'm so unhappy! It is true that I don't have any fun in my life.

It seems I remember liking to look at things, objects, like at the Pic n' Save. Seeing a lot of images, objects... do I like to do that? Like in stores, just seeing stuff? A lot of stuff?

Being at the ocean?

But I can't do that, no ocean around here.

I need to have some, I need to bring some fun into my life.

What is fun to me?

I don't have any fun!

I don't even know what fun is.

I have no idea where I would go to have fun.

Is writing fun?

I don't know. No. Yes. Maybe. I don't know. That's not what I mean.

A certain kind of writing is fun?

Is artistic writing fun?

This is much too complicated now and, therefore, over.

I shy away from too much complication as it saddens me, the inward knotting, after awhile I end that.

To have fun I will think of some things I can do to have fun, and then I will do them.

I don't even know what fun is!

Dear No One,

I am tired of being mistreated. I deserve better. I am very hurt, very abused. I often think "If this is how life is going to be, then I don't want to live." I hate my life. I am just waiting to die really. I hate the human race. Like Jean Rhys, I think people are cruel. Abominable. "Treacherous." Not being suicidal, I live on anyway. Living is just another one of the things I haven't chosen. I didn't choose to be born, I won't choose to die. Life is like that, and death too-- just things forced upon me, without my having any say. If I had been asked, I would have said "No. I do not want to be born." Life is not a good thing to me. It seems that it could have been a good thing but people are cruel. That's what it is. Cruel people have ruined life. I am like Rhy's Marya. Marya seems to me one of her most sad characters. Marya is very sad and she says so. I am 44 years old now and my heart can no longer heal. My mind is healed but my heart will never heal. How can it when it is being constantly bombarded? One of the reasons that my heart will never heal is that the cruelty persists. I no longer even try to heal my heart. I just try to avoid and minimize the most crushing blows. I try not to let the cruel people destroy me any more than they already have. Much more cruelty could kill me, could end my life completely. Since my heart can no longer heal, each cruel person, each cruel behavior pushes me closer to my death. I am very sad. I am too sad to live really but I live on. I have made it up to the last chapter of <u>Quartet</u>, by Jean Rhys. I am completely miserable. Men and women have almost destroyed me. I wonder why I have been the one destroyed. Because I let them? Because I would not stand up for myself? Because they knew they could kick me around and get away with it because I have no one to protect me? No one on my side. Yes, why have I been the one destroyed? A good question, that. Why have men and women aimed their weapons at me? Even men and women I have done nothing to. I think it is just their selfishness. I truly hate the human race. Men and women are selfish and cruel. I hate the human race and I have to live. What a cruel life! I hate my life. I hate the life I have. As Marya said, I hate "the sort of life" I have. I will finish reading the Rhys book, gather them all together like a meeting-- I hate that word!-- of all her parts of herself, tie a bow around the Rhys books, I have read many, if not all, of her books. Her striking intelligence. Then I will read Colette. I like her a lot. I will read her writing about her mom's house, I guess.

I am dying in my heart. Despair is ending my life. I do not think I can hold on much longer. This kind of life is not worth living. This kind of life is purposeless and meaningless. I began to write "Life is not worth living." But that is not it. It is this kind of life that is not worth living. This kind of life. If this is the kind of life that I am going to have, if this is how life is going to be... My life is over really. Oh blah blah blah.

Today is Friday. I have a Ratso Rizzo life! What I mean by that is that the Ratso Rizzo character is an accurate physical manifestation of/parallel to my corresponding emotional life. He accurately, physically manifests the condition of my emotional life.

My name is not Ratso... or somesuch quote... The name thing... thanks to a philosophy book, I understand.

My life is over. I like death because in death there is no emotional pain and hurt. I do not like all dead people though because they are just the end of what they were when they lived.

I could have a character, Death. What would Death do today? What does Death want to do? I guess Death could just do what everyone else does. Death could just be like everyone else. Death could go to the beach and get a tan. For what purpose? Enjoyment? To enjoy time?

The purpose of life is happiness.

My heart is dying.

I've turned into nothing but a big tear. That is all I am now, a big tear.

Let us now study this tear? Through research. And the act of crying, what is involved, how it happens.

No article in encyclopedia on Crying but some words in the dictionary section about tears. (The definition of crying will be in the dictionary instead of the encyclopedia, also synonyms.) Tears. My eye research?

Have you ever seen a Nazi's handwriting?

Just a thought.

Tears are just the fluids that come from the lacrimal glands. They contain salt, sodium bicarbonate, protein and others. Aside from an expression of emotion, tears have other functions. Tears give the eyes a bath and protect them. Tears come out when "...the muscles around the lacrimal glands tighten...". (quote from child encyclopedia.)

I am very unhappy. I am very sad. Specifically?

I am hurt very much. I should just go away and die. I wonder, who was the saddest person who ever lived? I don't think I can live much longer. I am dying of despair. My emotional pain is becoming unbearable. I am so hurt that I am barely able to function.

I have finished reading <u>Search For A Method</u>, by Jean-Paul Sartre. According to Sartre, the philosophy of Marxism is very important and provides a way for understanding many parts of modern life. Existentialism and Marxism provide a thorough understanding. Many things about modern life are understood as one reads. Some of the things I learned are that it is wrong to get rid of the particular, that psychoanalysis can be just the history of an individual, that Marxism puts an end to the "fetishism of interiority" (psychoanalysis), and that human beings are not, as is commonly said, "human resources" but, instead, "Pro-jects of comprehension." Sartre asks what the purpose is of being in the depths of subjectivity and what is "the real in subjectivity." He defines existence as moments of comprehension. Instead of psychoanalysis (Marx's "fetishism of interiority") one could understand a person in several ways-- "historical materialism," whether the person has his own tools or not (which is a social class determinate) or by one's "class ideology" (ideas of a social class.) He also writes of a new kind of achievement, "achievement of awareness" and writes that analyses is just a "synthetic reconstruction." Marxism is very important. The philosophy of Marxism is more important in understanding modern life than people think. It provides us with an understanding of many of the structures, realities, and occurrences of modern life. Marxism provides an understanding for many of the things that happen in our regular life. Marxism provides the reason why some of the seemingly unfathomable things occur.

On Wednesday night, I had "psychical phenomenon." The philosopher Edmund Husserl studies what the "psychical phenomenon" is. He understands precisely what happens during "psychical phenomenon." He writes on 106 of <u>Phenomenology and the Crisis of Philosophy</u> that "The psychical is divided (to speak metaphorically and not metaphysically) into monads that have no windows and are in communication only through empathy." Edmund Husserl states that there is no "external causality" "in the realm of the psychic." (Those quotes are from footnote 46, from the person who wrote the introduction, I suppose.)

When the "psychical phenomenon" occurs, Husserl is there, with his mind, understanding the structure of the psychical phenomenon and its other characteristics? No, that's it because I think he says that the phenomenon "knows no real parts,...". Anyway, he studies the "psychical phenomenon" "in and for itself."

I never am happy. I am never happy. What for me I have called despair and sadness, when it occurs, is for Husserl "psychic phenomenon" and he studies what this is (106, 107.) Instead of being in despair, in sadness, and all the other ways of saying, one can say one is in "the psychical sphere." Edmund Husserl studies the life inside that sphere.

These are writings on nonhistoric individuality; writings in ["is." (am).]

I am an individual.

I am a paragrapher.

I am thinking that my body has 2 of most things, and a type of body that would have 1 of the two and two of the one.

chest

internal organs
1 lung
2 hearts
2 stomachs
2 livers
1 kidney
2 brains

chest

I draw pictures sometimes. I think of pictures sometimes. When I don't think through a picture, I don't always draw the picture but sometimes I draw the thought picture.

I read. While I read, I think. Thoughts I have are about some, if not all, of the things I buy and own that have California in them somehow. What order things are in does not really matter.

My thoughts are based upon my reading. My thoughts have my reading as their foundation.

I am educated.

I am educated by reading and then my thoughts further my education.

The places where things are located might be a part of the things? My avocado oil is on the bookshelf.

I am sitting at my desk.

I am thinking of Socrates and during the writing of my short story when I was about 35 years old, I could not discern things.

I am 44 years old now.

Socrates is a proper name.

I comprehend names.

I am reading the things I wrote down.

Questions are not formed in the right way.

In society, the use of names is wrong. Wrong information is given by society. The participants in society do not understand the names.

I sense that names have no right meaning. In society, names are misused.

Oversimplification often occurs.

I think of my good professor often.

I am not reading Plato this night.

I see that in Plato ideas become individuals.

My paintings are--

"Writing on Canvas," "Aristotle," "The Scholar," "A Thinker" "Waterheart."

My inventions are A heart shield (1991,) A tear counter (1992, water sensitive object applies to cheek,) A pretty picture machine (1992,) "Stupid Spray" (1995, to keep stupid people away from me,) An Abuse-o-meter (1995,) The anguish machine and skis for shopping carts ("shopping sleds" for winter shopping.)

The End

Innocentia's Dream Classes

"I am awfully lonely," she said to no one.

"In order to cheer myself up, I will think of all the years I have to live; all the paid debts; all the quietness; my pretty clothes; food that I like to eat."

("I do not find power at all attractive. It scares me.")

"My pretty clothes (I am okay now, despite what others say or think about me) (I wonder, is it true, as I used to say when I was young, 'Men want just one thing?') (I'm sure a lot of people hate me. But I don't hate them and that is what has always made everything so weird) are things I like to touch and things I like touching me because they feel good touching my skin.

I am conservative, by nature.

I have finished reading <u>Miss Lonelyhearts</u> by Nathanael West and the poems of Robert Browning. Of course one never finishes with the work of such men's souls. I am just grateful that their souls can be with me for my whole life.

I am The Victim of Everyone.

The food that I like to eat (Life, after all, is the most important thing) is the food that I learned to eat at the university.

"A university gives one permission to mature into as much intelligence as one can," she said. "I have finished reading <u>The Day of the Locust</u>. I am reading <u>Brave New World</u>."

*   *   *

21

When I first met Professor Robert Browning, the reality of the scholarly life was shown.

With a certain unmistakeable, bearded seriousness, he stood before the class of 30 university students.

I think that, perhaps, he did not know that he was a great scholar. He was simply teaching. He was simply doing what he was paid to do.

Professor Browning's class was like a city, except that a few things, like swimming pools, were missing. (Classrooms and cities are similar in many ways.)

I noticed that, on the window sill, there was a sculpture and it was titled, "1,000." I do not know what it meant and I did not ask him. His temperament made one feel "Everything's O.K." His temperament made one feel that one belongs in the world and that the world is a good place.

His temperament made one feel "There will be room for everyone."

I was happy to be in his regular class. He nourished me. I was happy not to be excluded anymore. For the first time in my life I felt like I had a place in The Great Book of Life-- even if I was just an apostrophe.

Once he had another professor come and "sit in," as they call it, on the class.

(The Visiting Professor recently published "A soft towel" and "Breakfast is ready!"-- 2 works of scholarship regarding (1) what "things" are and (2) how a human being might begin a day. He was paid $1,000 and $2,000, respectively, for the "articles," as they are called.)

(It was also said that the Visiting Professor spoke 42 languages.)

The day the Visiting Professor visited, I was fortunate enough to be there (even though my hair was still wet and my legs had been too hastily shaven.) They had the following aulipheyius conversation:

(Professor Browning) "I understand that Professor Kant has become immeasureably wealthy."

(Visiting Prof) "As I have heard; that is to say, I have heard likewise."

(Browning) "And to think, his work is completed each day at 11:20 A.M."

(VP) "That is so, as I have heard, likewise."

(Browning) "It is said that he is awaiting patents on a new kind of toothpaste, and a new musical instrument; that he has redesigned the nation's transportation schedule, has come to a full understanding of the unconscious and has figured out what to do on Saturdays.

(VP) "I understand that he has also written brilliant articles on 'The Last Minute,' 'What's For Dinner?' and--"

(Browning) "Do you still like Mexican food?"

(VP) "What is Mexican food?"

(Browning) "That's a good question."

(VP) "It is a certain kind of food, isn't it?"

(Browning) "I don't know."

(VP) "Is it a complete kind of food? Is it satisfying?"

(Browning) "I think so."

(VP) "Then, let's have some."

Their conversation ended and Professor Browning's class was dismissed for the day.

*   *   *

The Victim of Everyone walked into one of the university's buildings.

It was morning.

She felt healthy because what she felt was the most important part of her, her brain, was becoming an unshakeable structure.

Her thoughts became clear. Each day the clarity increased. The despair that had clouded her brain and heart for her entire life was finally dissipating.

Her brain's system was beginning to resemble a university's structure.

"The university building makes sense for me because it resembles my thoughts," she said. "The room size seems correct. The arrangement of furniture seems correct. The places that the human beings occupy seems correct."

The Victim of Everyone walked noiselessly across the room's expanse. Students sat slouched, reading in several of the soft-looking chairs. Some students from a different country sat on the university's couch and discussed one scholarly issue or another. The building's windows reached from the floor to the ceiling.

She walked up to the food area that was located inside the warm building.

She placed her briefcase full of academic work on the floor.

"I'll have a large coffee," she said.

The food service worker gave her a large coffee.

Then, surveying the do-nuts, The Victim of Everyone chose one.

"I'll have the cinnamon donut, please," she said.

The food service worker gave her the cinnomen donut.

"That'll be $1.04," the food service worker said.

The Victim of Everyone paid for her breakfast in exact change.

"Thanks," she said to the food service worker.

(1) The Victim of Everyone didn't have anything else to say to the food service worker. (2) If she had anything else to say to the food service worker, she would have said it.

The Victim of Everyone took the coffee off of the counter with her left hand. With her right hand, she took two or three napkins from the silver napkin box. Also with her right hand, she took the donut off the counter.

With the donut and napkins in her right hand, and the coffee in her left, The Victim of Everyone bent down and grasped the handle on her briefcase with her right hand. She carried the donut and napkins in between her thumb and first finger of her right hand and held the briefcase handle with her remaining 3 fingers of her right hand.

With the breakfast in hand(s,) The Victim of Everyone walked noiselessly back past the reading and discussant students, and the windows that reached from the floor to the ceiling, and left the university building.

The Victim of Everyone sat on one of the university's curbs and ate her breakfast.

It was about 98 degrees. The coffee was about 150 degrees. The donut was about 40 degrees.

I have to get my work done, she thought, while munching her brown and white donut. I have to finish reading <u>Pnin</u> and <u>Murphy</u>.

*   *   *

When I first met Professor James A. A. Joyce I thought Real life is the most important thing.

CHAPTER THREE

Exercise 904

Professor James A. A. Joyce

"As everyone knows, the more brains one has, the less need for fancy equipment."

"Real brains use very rudimentary tools."

"I always know it's 1:00 on Saturday, not from a clock or calendar, but because major league baseball is on tv every Saturday at 1:00. That's also how I know that it's spring."

Such was the conversation among a few of the students as they awaited the professor.

A few of the students' thoughts, inaudible of course, as thoughts are were (1) I want him to start class on time because I don't like false promises (2) I paid good money for this class. I wish he would hurry up and (3) I should've stayed home and played the tuba instead.

Having just finished <u>Finnegan's Wake</u>, Professor Joyce drove (on higher ground, of course) one of his two Rolls Royces (Joyce's Royces he called them) to the pradalatius university and parked in one of the faculty lots (lot 6348934DNWUQ, to be precise.)

Humming an old Irish ballad, he scuttled into class.

"Rstyqin class!" he boomed and beamed.

The students coalesced into a gigantic question mark.

From somewhere deep inside me, I saw myself crying and feeling afraid. I was crying and saying, "please, Don't make me go!"

Then I heard a kind voice say "You don't have to go if you don't want to."

*   *   *

All the times I am forced to choose between loneliness and getting hurt, I usually choose lonesomeness.

I have finished reading <u>One Hundred Years of Solitude</u>.

*   *   *

The classy class day in the classroom was classy.

After making sure that all the students who were included in the classy class list were safely situated in prefunctional postures, class began.

And what a day it was!

Four years later, they all hung their black cords on the side of their hats and graduated, including me.

*   *   *

Before graduation, however, education was earned.

Telephoneless hours, (days, weeks, months and years) passed in study. Immersed in the lofty ideals of the greatest living and dead minds (a complete break with tradition) the students still found their way to food.

*   *   *

Professor James A. A. Joyce's mid-term class was a myiethatopicx study regarding the romantic tone of certain colors.

"Now what!" an exasperated student cried out.

Professor Joyce continued unequoxically, or unequoxically continued, either way, it didn't matter to him, his prefunciolical lecture regarding certain colors. In other words, he ignored him.

Professor Joyce explained that the color of beige contains the expression "I miss you."

*   *   *

After the mid-term term (the "after" is a nice word to keep this story chronological-- a story doesn't have to be chronological but it's okay if it is. Life is chronological so, in that sense, this story is realistic.) Professor Joyce said all he had to say one day and then dismissed the class.

That day, all of the students, including me, did the laundry.

With bright, clean clothes, we were all back in our seats for the next class.

*   *   *

"Sehyrila, class!" Professor Joyce said one morning (by way of greeting our changing minds.)

All of the students, including me, did their/our/hour best to understand.

"That's enough for today," Professor Joyce said. That is how the lecture began.

He ended the lecture that day with an introductory remark.

All of the students, including me, did their/our/thour (or theirur) best to understand.

*   *   *

"One day the paint brush," Professor Joyce said/and the lecture continued right along, thusly.

The watercolors, sized 8 or 7½, some canvasses and curried rice, steamed vegetables, all the watercolors, the paint brushes,

I love you I love you;

check the rhythm

there, My Love, how does it sense,

I love you I love you--

it's stupid! It's the

part that's-- it's nervous, very
nervous, a very nervous laugh, no, not nervous so much,
nervous, a nonsensical word-- means nothing! What does
that mean afterall--nervous? No one knows, it's one of those
popular words that everybody likes but nobody knows what
it means but it goes around anyway and everybody ends up
saying words that they don't even know what they mean --

An A student chimed in at this point.

"Many of us are far away from home," he said.

"My feelings hurt," a second student said.

Professor James A. A. Joyce continued.

Healing rhythms, healing rhythms...

And so, Professor James A. A. Joyce began, in an
unassuming classroom, a healing of The World Mind.

*   *   *

When the semester nearly closed, Professor James A. A.
Joyce and I designed a tutorial.

I began formal study with him the following fall.

We decided to begin in the fall because fall seems to me
the most academic time

*   *   *

(Tutorial, Monday, September)

"You and your husband have a daughter, I see. You are a bit older than the average student," he said.

"Older inside as well, Professor," I said.

"You and your husband's daughter, when first she spoke--" he said.

"She said 'appu juice' for apple juice."

"The language you and your husband's daughter speaks retains, is all-important in my view," he said. "That is because you and your husband's daughter's language is like my own. What other words did she say?"

"Her first words were often about nourishment. Her speech, perhaps, had a practical reason for being. She spoke to tell me the foods she wanted to eat. I suppose that is a very good justification for speech and its importance?" I asked.

"I will see you on Wednesday," he said.
(Tutorial, Wednesday)

"The formal Study of Language is where we begin today," he said.
"Let us begin."

"Formal language is something like 'One understands and loves the ocean,'" I said. "'One studies worlds' oceans.' 'One's nature is drawn to oceans.' And so on."

Professor Joyce reached for his notebook. His notebook was on the top shelf of his desk. He opened his notebook. He took a pen from his shirt pocket.

"For Friday you are to write the ocean in the formal style," he said.

He closed his notebook.

???somehow. Maybe I'll go and apply for that job at the business office. It seemed like an interesting prospect.) Sometimes I wonder what it would be like to live in another country.

- The ocean has been misused, he said. Is that why you are drawn to the ocean?

- No.

- Why then? Why do you like the ocean so much?

- Maybe because it is healthy, I said, I swim there and it's fun, there's a whole world of good feelings and thoughts there, healthy, maybe that's why and also maybe it doesn't matter why it is just that I love it so that is all about it, it is just that I love it and so that is all.

I would understand the ocean as unbroken, as A lifegiving Unbroken, he said.

- Cognition.

- The ocean near your young life, he began-- I imagine moments of full happiness there, seeing the sandcrabs, checking the dates for when the grunion are running, walking upon the cold rocks of the jetty one morning, seeing the lifeguard tower, running along the water's edge, back and forth between the wet sand and the dry, these happy memories, what is to become of them...

- We had a fun night once near and in the water, at the beach, at night. We swam at night. It was fun and exciting, I don't know what else to say about it except that it was fun and

- Do not underestimate language, he said. There are things to say about it, always, whatever the subject.

- Ok, well, so, there was a boy there but I was very young, and just for a few moments, and anyway, I am sure he would be very angry if he knew...

- Ah well, the forbidding feelings! he said. No matter. Let's move on to something else. Perhaps at the upcoming Tutorial we will sit alongside each other as if we are taking a drive thru some distant city, in Ireland, perhaps!

Tutorial, Wednesday

(I) - Sometimes the words come out all wrong

(he)- the rhythm of the words, that is where the problem and solution is, the rhythm of the words, sentences, paragraphs, pages, chapters, books, how one goes to the other and all of that you see, Classical Rhythms

(I) Many of the things I have been taught are wrong

(he) hmmm?

(I) These... glytupidul moralities that rain down from God knows where, it's as if so many things are supposed to bother me, all kinds of residue-type words in my mind, but my feelings don't really correspond to those moralities, like lying, for instance, it doesn't really bother me when someone lies but there are Residue Words in my mind that always tell me it should bother me, etc., but it doesn't really, it's kind of like Well, if that's what that person wants to say...

(he) Yes, if that's what that person wants to eat, if that's what that person wants to read...

(I) Some of the language from my ocean home, some explanations and words are 'The Point" which is not a philosophical inquiry to me, it is a real place at the beach, "The Point," a great place for surfing, it is a place, a physical place with all its descriptions, 'The Cross' also is a place, a little farther from the beach, up on a hill, one place where young men and women "park" as they call it which, for some strange reason, really means kiss and hug and on from there and so sometimes I feel as if I speak a different language, even though it is English, because of where I grew up and all the places and buildings I've known.

Tutorial, Friday

So many scattered notes, I said.
They are all tied together, brought together here, he said.
The despair of the past--I said
Gives way to the joy of the preseet, he said.
George Orwell--
Cerebral, he said. The essays are the intellect, his gift from God.
My memory seems able--I said.
Hmmm? he asked.
I remember 5 years ago so clearly. And portions of my very early life. After all, my early life was academic, I have always been academic.

(he) (Laughing.) I see that!

(I) When I think of being loved and cared about I think of my teachers and professors. I have had some really good teachers and professors. I think they really cared about me. I have had some really good teachers and professors.

(he) Thank you.

(I) Sometimes I read law books, for fun in a way. To study. To study, I think, the meaning and to try and figure out the abstract ideas which I think law is partly about, maybe. The ideals.

(he) Sometimes things... things have been harsh, but they will not be harsh anymore, not to you. There is no more harshness.

(I) I study.

(he) (Laughing.) I see that! You have your pencils and notebooks, there is no shortage.

(I) That's right.

(he) Then, let us begin. For Monday--

(he) Then, let us begin. For Monday--

(he) Then, let us begin. For Monday--

(Paper for Professor James A. A. Joyce,
In preparation for Monday tutorial,
Language Studies in formal Prose)

I am The Victim of Everyone, real life is the most important thing, healing rhythms, I am The Victim of Everyone, real life is the most important thing, the High IQ, the "intelligence quotient," such a thing as that, "intelligence quotient, cerebral! A marriage, a good life, a With this ring, a true love, a top priority, a pleasing, a pleez-zing, how does it seem, a healing rhythm, a dream, a dr-eee-mmm, how does it seem, it senses well, it senses fine, on the money! It looks well, it looks fine, Forcing Peace, it seems fine, real life, it seems okay, For me, For Myself, it seems fine, the healing, the h-e-el-ling, rhyth-mmms, rhyth-mmms, the ocean is within reach, it seems fine, it seems okay, indeed, we will watch, w-aaa-ch, we will understand, we will laugh, we will feel, at all the ocean things, throwing a pail of water on the events of the day, see, what appropriate distance, what objective narration, the beach towel, the sides, draping, all the enclosed areas, where are all the people before the day begins, begin, in preparation, in preparation for, one can not simply be in preparation, one must be in preparation for, see the jellyfish named Afraid Of, sitting in school, beforetime, In The Beforetime, he forgot to bring his writing paper, or else he did not forget to bring his writing paper, writing with one's life, I suppose, that day, writing with one's priceless body, such a comfort, a weakness occurs, healing rhythms, as a wader enters, the jellyfish and the wader, they do not speak to each other, they only seem to emphasize, m--faa-seyes, emphasize one to each, each other, "ULLLLL" the jellyfish said, simply ULLLL the troubled world, the world mind, on its way, no matter the sunburn, it feels good, it tightens my skin, the water cools me off, the ocean heals my soul.

Does it make sense, after all, we are not so imbecilic, it is not as if things are not intellectual, the studious, the scholarship, what does it all mean, it is not as if there is no vigorous intellect, upward, onward, the meaning of things, the intellect, the intelligence quotient, what does it all mean, all this ocean water, so active! The ocean heals my soul, I "go in" as it is called "up to my waist." Yes, I Go In Up To My Waist, I do not simply go, how incomplete that may seem, what I do is Go In Up To My Waist, I have longed to hear, I have longed to h--e--eerr, I have longed for some kinds of words that have not been placed together for many years, I have longed for some kinds of words that have not been placed together for many years, "I go in up to my waist," I am not so certain as I once was that I may write with a pen and never look back, as if erasers are not needed, erasers are needed, I don't know if they are needed, it is that I need them, I like them, I have not yet read, I have not yet, I want to read The Master of Go, written by someone, and The Erasers by Alain Robbe Grillet, the ocean heals my soul, the water coo-oo-lls, the water is good for me, the ocean heals my soul, "I go in up to my waist," the ocean is never lonely, it does not hurt me, the ocean never hurts me, it feels good on my forehead, I'd say the ocean is about 50°, there are days when that is not true, the ocean heals my soul, the water feels good for me, "I go in up to my waist," a feeling of stictness, "I go in up to my waist," I have not yet come to understand the book The Marquis Went Out at 5, I would like to read that particular one, That Particular One, there are some things, the jellyfish mentioned earlier, the wader, "I go in up to my waist," a spirit, the ocean heals my soul, I wish part of me would stop running off and being lost, Somehow, that is a word for me, Somehow, that jellyfish doesn't bother me, the salt water stiffens my hair, isn't my hair important, I am The Victim of Everyone, it seems as if the world's movie camera has been focussed on the wrong people, and all the bad people have become the celebrities while all the kind people just quietly die off, the focus of the world's camera, where should the attention be paid, I am sure we must ask Immanuel Kant about that but I am told he is quite busy, sometimes things that are not desirable one day are desirable another, and they are not called moods, as is commonly thought, the feelings are not called moods, you see, moods is not a word for me, as Somehow is, yes, Somehow is a word for me, the feelings are not called moods, as is commonly thought, the feelings are needs. They are called needs, ne-e-e-dz. I go in up to my waist, I am The Victim of Everyone, the world focus has been pointed at the wrong person, my hair is important, how "I wear my hair" as it is said, I am certain it is more plausible to understand it thus, My hair is important, my intelligence quotient is one hundred and ninety, you will be always be by my side, forever, these are some words for me, as Somehow is a word for me, these are some words for me, the horses that run on the racetracks in California are very beautiful, the ocean heals my soul, the gentleness softens, is he your classmate? I suppose it may be true, the classroom seems to have been the most comfortable place for me, these are some words for me, as Somehow is a word for me, a w--errr-d, Somehow is an understanding for me, a gentleness softens, I am the victim of Everyone, it seems fine, the simple These are nice books, it will be all right, the Victim of Everyone, these are nice words, as Somehow, Everything is fine, as Somehow, I go in up to my waist, Everthing is fine, real life is the most important thing, I am the Victim of Everyone.

Tutorial, Monday

"We will happily marry 'the healing words' and 'the healing images,' Professor James A. A. Joyce said. "You are happy and healthy in life. You are safe and free from worry. Though the world may stumble or fall, you will not. You will be loved always and everything is okay."

Professor James A. A. Joyce made the sign of the cross.

When I first met Professor Charles Dickens, I was standing near a wall that was made of all wood. I was appropriately dressed. I was wearing a suit. I was looking out into the courtyard, as I often did. It was a warm, bright day.

Professor Dickens gave one a feeling before he gave one any concrete reality. His presence, placed into words, was "I will help you."

After I received his first gift of feeling, he gave another: Laughter.

"I am a comical writer," he said. I could understand that his laughter was fully-realized. I could understand that his laughter was the result of his having understood all the sadness in life.

"Enjoy life!" he said. "And Merry Christmas!"

Then, he walked out of the apartment. He closed the door softly behind him.

The superlative Professor Sherlock Holmes was another matter entirely. Here was a man of the first water. A Summa Cum Laude of life! An intellectual pinnacle! A regular Mount Everest of the mind!

As previously stated, he was superlative.

*   *   *

I was busy practicing my french ("Je vais bien," "Tiens!" "Veux-tu que nous allions?" "Bonjour, Madame," "Ils se sont regarder," "tant que vous en auriez vouler," "l'epaule," "Quelle heure est-il?" "pendant, pendant des jours, pendant une heure," "le cahier," "a la casse," "la blanchisserie," "se plaindre," "le decollete," "ne... personne," "ne... plus," "ceinture de securite," "heure de pointe," "le clignotant," "le coin," "combien font," "ne... pas," "sage," "comme ca," "la coup plus naturelle," "lavable," "mari," "les meilleurs") when a knock came at the door.

With this thought in mind, "smog!" I answered the door.

*   *   *

I was wearing pedal pushers, a top with rickrack, a diamond necklace, and go-aheads. My hair was shoulder-length, parted on the side and of changed-color.

*   *   *

It was a redoubtable Wednesday. The day began in full capacity.

"Brainwaves are like ocean waves," I thought.

Professor Sherlock Holmes stepped into the apartment.

After quickly sizing up the apartment, he walked to one of the walls. He pulled a chair to the space and said: Mind if I sit here.

There was no question or question mark.

Holmes sat and crossed one leg over the other.

"Let's see the ideas" he said.

I sat next to him, as he requested. I think that's what he requested when he said "let's."

He said something.

I said "I would rather write as a way to know you, than speak."

"Sometimes the words don't come out right," he said.

"I think so," I rejoined.

"Write, therefore!" he said.

He smiled.

"I will read it," he said. "That is how best to know you. You like to be able to erase right away, title, and restate in a correct form what you wish to speak. What do you want to say to Professor Holmes."

Again, no question and no question mark.

"I feel threatened by people who accomplish things that I can not even aspire to, it really hurts me. I feel as one feels when corruption occurs on a sacred day.

I feel far from home, like one slab of concrete forced into place. Then another."

I handed Mr. Holmes the writing. Without looking at it, he slid it into his book bag.

He stood up.

"I must be leaving now," he said.

Neither of us said good bye because we both knew that there have already been enough good byes said to last a lifetime.

"Mr. Holmes acknowledges 'Hello' only," he said.

Placing the shoulder strap of his book bag over his right shoulder, he walked briskly out the door.

Ah well, to study my french, to keep my intellect at optimum, a figure, paindre, avant tout, l'apres midi, (appeared, to paint, before all, afternoon) rappelez, l'air, l'hiver, le printemps (to remember, appearance, winter the springtime) la librairie, longent, soif, la faim, mentir le couteau, dur our dure, flanent, a ce moment la, passionnait pour, poussint, au bout de, chauffage (the bookstore, walk along, thirsty, hunger, to lie, knife, hard, strolling, then, liked well, are growing, at the end of, furnace.)

I am reading <u>Man's Fate</u>, by Andre Malraux.

I was thinking about a rare human quality today, loyalty.

I have been thinking about giving up my romantic view of life. That would be a big change for me. It would be sad to give up such a view.

I have also been thinking of writing the job description for what it means to be Mrs. The job of Mrs.

It may not be right to give up the romantic view. That would have magnanimous consequences. The failure of love and romance amongst the professionals... Oft' times... though, it feels that I am fighting a losing battle; that I should just say Forget it. Maybe love and romance could survive that, but I don't know. The demands that would be placed upon me by other careerists may break the love and romance. Since so many of the careerists are themselves anti-love, anti-romantics, and all ambition, careerists would certainly be toxic influences on me. Why are most people so anti-love, anti-romantic? Because of their personal qualities? Their love of money? Probably their love of money and power. It makes me sad that those are the values of the careerists.

Still, I find myself alone in this view. I feel sort of like a lone hold-out for a dying cause, with all the so-called successful people saying "Oh, how quaint" or "Isn't that sweet" in their nasal, cynical ways, as they buy up the houses and cars. The careerists seem perfectly happy. They don't feel that their hearts are hardened. Hardening of the emotional arteries of the heart. That describes what people glibly call Contemporary Society. Can't you just hear a professional woman saying Con-temp-or-rary-y So-ci-ett-ty.

Come to think of it, I'm not sure that the heart has arteries? But anyway, you get the idea.

And some people are so confident! That's the funny part-- confident and dead wrong!

Anyway, who am I to say anything about so-ci-ett-tyy anyway! I'm no culture specialist!

I just want to be happy. Being happy used to be easy. I guess when people so-called grow up (Do they really? Do people really change that much? How many people do you know who really progress?) they forget what happiness is. It used to be so easy! I started out happy, as a kid. I am happy, as an adult. That's logic!

But there's always a careerist, "Oh, that's so infantile!" she'll say.

Infantile I am, then.

But I will be happy.

Regarding the Andre Malraux book, manuscript, treatise (On your marks, get set, go!) or textual exposition-- how these artificial lights bother me, think I'll turn the artificial overhead light off-- the book is set, or "takes place" as it is said, in China. The city most written about is Peking.

(That may be wrong. What is this anyway-- a quiz?) Suffice it to say, the book is set in China.

Some of the writing in dialogue is written in the accent of a Chinese-speaking person. It shows what it would sound like if this person speaks English.

As often happens in writing, there is another something which needs to be written here.

It is about six o'clock P.M. and so I must close for the day.

I am the Victim of Everyone.

Real life is the most important thing.

I am the Victim of Everyone.

The other something that needed to be written was The Good...

Why DID the chicken cross the road? Really?

Such are the great mysteries that have boggled the best minds of humankind since time immemorial. That says something about "the best minds," huh.

"...When I look back on my life..." (sigh) (comma) "...I have defined certain terms..." (comma) plans, talk, and blahblahblah, Septembers, bedrooms, sometimes I wonder what will become of me. Do you? "Home life" is a nice sounding word, homelife. Homelife is a nice sounding word, isn't it. "Quietly packing my things"-- that seems true, like a true thing to say, it sounds true, listen, "Quietly packing my things." Quietly packing my things. "Wallet" doesn't sound nice, listen, "wallet." Is there another word for the compartment or enclosed carrier that men place their things in. The sound of words, "coupons"-- arggh! "Glasses" sounds nice. The way one speaks, "allowed,"-- what of that one, "allowed"? "Tables." How is this, "What are you doing?" "Nothin'." "Stuff." What of this-- "List below all the..."? "Such and such 'emanates' from him; Such and such 'is apparent'"-- what of those? Quietly packing my things, "Nothing could be farther from the truth." "Oh?" (comma) or "longing for"? These things, these ways of saying, "purposefully," and ending with a "Bug off!" "Huh!" Spirited terms, I suppose, spirited. "Belittling," all this will receive a light touch, "Oh, I will broach the subject," ahem! "Broach" indeed. "Dominance," "small," "sport," "heart attack," "attack..." aa--taakk...(comma) "Oh 'I shall suggest' this or that," "broken my heart." That sounds true, broken my heart, you have broken my heart, so and so has broken her heart, "He thinks he's God's gift to women."! "Away," so and so is "away." Quietly packing my things, nothing could be further from the truth. That is a true thing to say, "Nothing could be further from the truth." "Mens' faces," what of mens' faces, what of them. "Definite lies," that is something true, "Definite lies." "My whole life..." (comma) "'My whole life' this or that," "My whole life."

I am The Victim of Everyone.

So it is, with probes.

What of "whilst," the way words sound, the "nothing could be further from the truth." What of "no end to," "the gains sought," the "much-revered"-- much-revered? What is that? "Nearly" this or that, what is a "false front"? Homelife sounds nice, homelife. "Touch," a sense of touch, "abjectly," "anywhere"-- anywhere, what is that, anywhere. "Places." "Abruptness." "jabs." Punching bags, wrecking balls, the "That is probably mostly true" or "Nothing could be further from the truth." "'No it aint!' 'Yes it is!" These are some words and phrases for study. "Everything." "The things I imagine."

I am The Victim of Everyone.

As mentioned earlier, or before-- if I am not mistaken, "earlier" and "before" have exact meaning, that is to say, same meanings-- I am reading <u>Man's Fate</u>.

My personal notes, and markings in the printed book, emphasize the novel's picturesqueness: rickshaws, jade, cactuses, wool sweaters, clothes with pockets and sake.

Sometimes, as a note on style, Andre Malraux breaks words in unprecedented places. Some words that are usually 2 words are made into one.

There are many similarities between Chinese political history and Jewish political history.

Two other themes of interest are Identity and Language. Part of the Chinese cultural malaise is caused by an individual's loss, lack of an individual identity. Identity-building is a real solution to a culture's or a country's ills or unrest. The language of the novel is political. Such terms as "consulate" and "insurrection" are used.

There are some studies of religion on about pages 160-170; some teachings about arts (190-197 or so) (comma) and some interesting thoughts on writing (198.) I also finally figured out one of the things that reading does. It brings back broken or forgotten parts of your life back to you. Whew! That was not easy to figure out!

I like to write with a fountain pen.

I like Descriptive Writing. Descriptive Writing Keeps me well and happy.

Professor Hart Crane had a structured, scholarly mind. The professor's intellection could be seen in process as he stood in front of the class, the first day of the semester. His vocabulary had been built-up and acquired through years of studying and reading. He was a living representative of the scholarly life.

The strident academic schedule, which began the first day of the semester, continued through the entire term: selected readings for close study, papers, tests, and exams.

For Professor Crane, the study and understanding of literature was as demanding as any subject of academia. Studying the work of the greatest minds of humankind was, indeed, Education in its true form.

*   *   *

The class began thus: Inclusionary building materials, in sequential form, provide an emphasis. I am over something, such forms state: The human soul is joyous.

*   *   *

The words Professor Crane spoke in one class, transcribed from my notes, were: "That's not my line of work" may be a helpful idea. One must not be burdened. The poems of Wordsworth are to be understood by Friday.

*   *   *

There was a quiz that Friday. I understood the poems of Wordsworth. I got an A.

*   *   *

The mid-term essay questions reminded me of a winter's day.

I did my best, beginning with an idea of the safe places-- safe emotionally-- inside of a poem.

The second question concerned the nature of a professorial mind and how such a mind could best profit in today's world.

*   *   *

There was a quiz on Wednesday. It involved descriptive writing about water. Since I had done that atleast a million times, I skipped the class.

I thought that day anyway. I thought: (1) Myopia abounds! and (2) being well-informed is overrated. I wondered what it means to be important and how one goes about becoming important.

I ended my day not knowing what to do with all the things I have done.

*   *   *

Professor Crane's final exam was comprehensive.

When I had finished "taking" (as it is termed) the exam, I "turned in" (as it is termed) my paper and left the class.

I am a quiet person, I thought.

Professor Crane was then firmly established in my heart and mind forever.

CHAPTER TWELVE

Language Studies

One day, while standing near a building, I had the following conversation with a person I did not know and would never see again after the conversation ended:

I: I never blame myself for anything. I never will.

he: Me either.

I: Do I have to keep writing I-he, he-I before every sentence? That's one reason I never wrote a play.

he: I think you have to unless we're always going to each speak in turn; you know, 1 for you, 1 for me.

I: Well, what happens if I interrupt you?

he: I guess you better just use the he, I, I, he format.

I: Okay.

he: Why'd you look at me like that?

I: Like what.

he: You gave me a weird look.

I: I don't know.

he: Can't you just answer the question?

I: Probably not.

he: Well then. You're the rudest person I've ever met.

I: Am not. And 'most rude' sounds better.

he: Okay. Most rude.

I: Another compromise. That's good.

he: Are we each just going to say 1 sentence each? If we each said more, then you wouldn't have to write the I, he, he, I so much.

I: Good idea! Would you like to launch into a soliloquy?

he: It may be termed a monologue?

I: Whatever.

he: I don't think so. Monologues get pretty lonely.

I: What do you want to talk about then?

he: How about current events?

I: Nah.

he: What about male-female relationships?

I: Nah. Overdone.

he: What then?

I: I don't know.

he: Maybe there's nothing to talk about.

I: may-BE.

he: Why do you talk like that, putting emphasis on certain parts of words? What's wrong with you anyway?

I: Nothing.

he: Then, why do you do that?

I: I don't know.

he: I'm going to stop asking you questions if you're gonna answer 'I don't know' to everything.

I: Okay.

he: Je ne sais pas is I don't know in French.

I: That's nice.

he: This is a boring play.

I: Yes it is. So, let's liven it up.

he: But how? And don't say I don't know.

I: Okay, I won't say that. I'll say this: Let me think for a moment.

he: That's better.

I: How to liven up this play...

he: We could end it, that would liven it up, just end it.

I: Maybe you're right, if being right is important. Maybe we should just end the conversation.

he: Here. I'll end it. You do it this way: Good bye!

I: Good bye.

he: Should I look back over my shoulder and say So long?

I: I don't know.

I am the Victim of Everyone.

I am almost 42 years old.

I have had 3 happy years in my whole life.

Certain words not in my vocabulary.

There is 1 person in the whole world who would care if I lived or died.

I am The Victim of Everyone.

The End

CRITICA'S OBSERVATIONS

The qyec monster crawls along the ground. It is moving toward me but I remain still. As I expected, Brona appears against the sky and pulls the qyec monster into her mouth. Brona bites off half his body then strangles him. The qyec monster typically underestimated another monster's strength. It made the mistake of putting too much emphasis on a monster's psyche. That a monster such as Brona is weird or incoherent may be correct. But Brona is not only that. In fact, she is barely that. Her incoherencies become immediately irrelevant when she has you in her mouth. The qyec monster might well have had a small satisfaction as she chewed him up. Perhaps he died knowing his theory correct. But he died nonetheless, in great pain. A true monster has no desire to be human and has no special taste for entrails. Brona eats things in their whole form and is still not satisfied. While the qyec monster was searching around for a small entrail, Brona destroyed him. The qyec monster might well have become human had he gotten hold of my entrails. I will never know. All I know is that he will never be allowed to because Brona, and all those like her, will eat him, and his kind, as a quick snack while they crawl around on the ground, looking for small treats. As the day passed, I saw Brona destroy the entire race of qyec. She ate every scout, aspirant, laborer and slave of the qyecian colony. They were attracted by my smell and each fell into Brona's fate. I watched her eat them one by one and, by the late afternoon, she no longer bothered to strangle them but swallowed them whole. The queen was the last to go. She kicked a bit more and, by the shutter Brona gave off when swallowing her, was probably more bitter than her friends.

Brona is female and, as far as I can tell, somehow descended from a race of monsters called Adya. She has Adyaian traits: long ears, awkward neck, salmon smoke. Brona (as all Adyaians) has infinitely mixed blood--is part monster, part giant, part myth. As typical Adyaian, her ancestry is mostly internal-- her psyche is mixed. She is young but as she ages, her physical traits will manifest her psyche and she will no longer resemble the Adyaian race at all. The entire scholarship on the Adayians is, of course, risky and suspect. However, her origins are not so important as her immediate danger. As her physical traits manifest her psyche, she has been mistaken for the muse but, in reality, she is no such thing. She is a simple menace, a bother. I will attempt first to observe her behavior and then I will destroy her. I no longer have the patience nor generosity of exile. Brona, and all those like her, will be destroyed. I will find her soft place and stab her there.

Brona walks to a far corner of Trella Park and heaves smoke from her belly. The smoke falls over the park, over my notebook and I suffer confusion. Who is she? I ask myself, I forget where I am, what my purpose is, I sense pulling toward and away and see her real danger: the cloud. As the smoke settles, I regain strength and set out on the journey of definition. Even as my sense of the present returns, my ability to recall her history is vague. It occurs to me that Brona is able to erase her own history. No matter, it isn't necessary to destroy her. Her present is evil enough, I have no need of her history. What can it matter to me where her ancestors dwelt? I willingly cross out my notes on her ancestry and move ahead without it. I can still, however, remember her name? Brona. That is all I need to go on, it is enough. I condemn her past to clouds, to unsupportable evidence, to loss. The present danger is all I need remain conscious of. I look through the bush leaves and see Brona wax sexless, then male, then female, then sexless. It is her evasive tendencies, her contradictions of persona--those are what I need remain aware of. She may, at once, deny her ancestry and become autonomous, no matter. I am able to call Brona She, He and It. No matter. All that needs doing is destruction.

Brona: perhaps she descends from Fedor? Perhaps she has grown from inside one of the boxes he liked to collect? Perhaps Fedor has not drowned himself as rumored? Questions of memory keep my nose in my notebook and I almost suffer the loss of my right arm as Brona steps over the bush. I vow never to look back, to let her origins disintegrate. I vow to protect myself now.

Brona leans over the sidewalk and vomits living forms, perhaps gives birth to baby Fedors or Adyas or any number of other weirdos but I can't get close enough to really see, I don't want to see. She straightens her back and stands looking down. She stands. Perhaps she carries them all inside her, perhaps I've witnessed a childbirth of aged forms but I can't get close enough to see, I don't want to. I watch Brona, I know she could destroy me quickly. I observe her hands, she rubs her chest then stretches her arms into the sky. Nothing happens. She lies down. Nothing happens, her eyes stay open. She begins calling someone, she screams Eftu Ppef! Eftu Ppef! A mating call? No, it doesn't have the whine of a mating call, what does she want? She waxes male and screams Tufp Ffep! I dutifully write the sound in my notebook and remain stable. He closes his eyes and turns to his side. He withdraws in great pain, his forehead wincing and clutching the bottoms of his feet, he shrinks. I wait for eleven hours. Brona remains small, holding his feet. He remains on his side. At the twelfth hour, Brona is female. In a weak cough, she spits a blue streak of liguid that falls on my hiding bush. The bush is gone and I know with certainty, Brona has no past. I know with certainty I must meet her as she is now and give up the foolish notion that she is somehow connected with something else. Her danger is too immediate.

Brona instantly gains an identity. She is most certainly female. She is a bit larger than human females, emits an odor that sickens me. She begins walking along the outside of the park collecting debris and stacking it. She makes five piles, arranges the piles from large to small. She continually glances over her shoulder toward the sky, then moves. She clears a portion of the park, pulling up the grass, smoothing the dirt then sitting there. She amuses herself in this way until daylight. At dawn, again, she waxes male, returns to her side, shrinks. She continues this pattern as a routine and I begin to sense her weakness: habit. I plan a disorder. I sense it is disorder she cannot tolerate. I observe her ritual one more full day and when she falls to sleep, I steal one piece of debris from her smallest pile. I am surprised when she awakes and doesn't seem to notice. I have underestimated her distraction. I try again, this time stealing two pieces from her large pile. She responds the same way. She passively replaces the missing pieces and I am touched by her humility. During her next sleep, I don't steal the debris but, instead, throw it into chaos. When she wakes, she begins to vomit and I sense a disturbance. It is not absence she cannot tolerate, it is chaotic presence. She sits looking down at the strewn debris and waxes sexless in an attempt to compensate. She changes form entirely, turns into a dragon and, in my notebook, I rename this form of her Dar. The dragon Dar begins muttering and shaking and changing color. Dar walks along the inside of the park touching shapes only it can imagine. I sense its inability to distinguish reality and step into the open. It brushes by me but does not touch me, seems content on touching only what does not exist. The murder of the dragon is child's play and I feel almost guilty. With a sense of minor regret, I walk to the dragon and drop poison into its mouth. Dar shivers a slight shiver, lies on the ground and dies a simple death. I take to hiding behind a tree and wait for my next challenge.

I must report now that Brona's presence has had its effects on me. There are moments now when my memory is weak. I have to look back over my notebook to recall her names and evolutions. I often forget whether she caused the bush I was hiding in to disintegrate or not and I am at a complete loss to distinguish which actions she performed while male, female or neither. I can only beg your patience and tolerance and ask you to keep in mind the more noble hope of this journey's conquest. If I, at times, return to a bush that is not there or fight a monster that has been previously destroyed, you must understand that contact with these beings does have its drawbacks. You must understand that a certain number of these diseases are contagious and even though I have taken every precaution against them, it is inevitable that I will be infected slightly. I have, of course, promised myself to remain as human as possible and if I do sense any beginnings of metamorphosis in my own person, I will withdraw from this project immediately. I only ask that you forgive me any inconsistencies in objects so that I will not have to trouble myself with them too much and I can get on with the more important aspects of this report.

Morven is about five-foot-nine and weighs over three hundred pounds. His hair grows as stiff bristles on only the top right side of his head. He has no other bodily hair. His face is perfectly circular and seems too large for the head. His arms have enormously developed muscles while his fingers are useless. Morven can lift large objects but cannot pick up smaller ones. For this reason, I am, for the time being, relatively safe from him. I don't know if Morven craves human flesh, I have seen him at meals only once and noticed that he consumed huge amounts of dust, soap and various other common household items. His mobility is somewhat feeble because he is propelled by several small feet that have grown from his shoulder blades. From his mid-back down, there are no feet so he is forced to drag himself along the ground being vulnerable to broken glass, stickers and any number of insects. I have read that a sting from a common red or black ant will cause Morven to swell twice his size, grow temporarily insane, sleep for three days straight then return to his normal state. I have, of course collected several ants and put them in a jar and they are fighting here by my knees. I don't want to use the ants on Morven and have captured them only for emergencies. I am interested in a more permanent destruction and here, the ants prove useless. Morven is moving toward the center of Trella Park and I am slightly amused at the sound of his locomotion. I sense an abundance of liquid in the monster for he sounds like tennis shoes walking through a lake. He has no apparent odor but does seem to have command of the english language, does seem to have the reasoning of an average American, does seem to have some knowlege of music. I step from behind the tree. Morven sees me at a distance and begins dragging himself over to me. I stand ten feet from him and notice his eyes looking at my legs. Apparently he has never seen a human being for he addresses my knees.

Wow it's so good to see you, he says, whataya been doin', did ya' vote in the last election? He reaches out to shake my hand. I decline and observe. He goes on: I just got back from Europe you know and what an experience! I mean, I really learned a lot, you know? Morven shakes his own hand and I begin to sense his peculiar communication mode. In a deeper voice he answers himself: Oh yeh? Like what, what did you learn? Well (Morven's voice switches back to the first one he used) I don't know exactly, just some sense of vastness, you know.

I'm not sure if Morven senses my presence at all. Can he suffer as Dar suffered? Does he talk to things that don't exist? I risk an approach. Morven, I say, I'm Sumiv (giving a false name) a human being. He shakes his own hand again and continues his jabber, continues his monologue in two voices. He doesn't seem to hear me. I look closely at his face and notice he does not have two ears but one that is slightly underdeveloped. I move close to the underdeveloped ear and repeat my introduction in a louder tone. As the vibrations enter his ear, his arm begins to swell slightly and liquid emerges from his mouth. He shows no signs of pain but does not communicate my language. I realize that communication with Morven cannot be verbal. I do not give up the idea of communication all together. Perhaps by touch? But where? As Morven continues to busy himself with self-talk, I reach to his back and touch one of the toes on his feet. A powerful sucking sensation, a vacume almost, pulls me into him and it takes all my strength to pull my hand back. The ends of my fingers burn and small blisters form. I retreat behind the tree and wait for my hand to heal. Within the hour, my hand resumes its normal shape and there seems to be no damage. I resolve, however, to strike Morven from the back somehow and sense that it is his feet he needs for survival. I am curious to see his reactions to music and I begin singing a song I learned as a child. Morven rolls to his stomach, making his back-feet more vulnerable. I must use a stick to jab him because I can't risk the loss of my hand. I break a branch from the tree and jab him once in the bottom of a foot. But instead of pain, the jab brings him pleasure equal to a human massage. I jab harder, he coos. I realize his back-feet are not capable of receiving pain and only capable of inflicting it. I must find the part of him that receives pain. I continue to jab around with the branch but get only baby gurgles. I must have overlooked something, there must be some spot, some idea, some action that will bring him pain. I try speech again.

But Morven continues to shake his own hand and talk to himself. I sense that his speech is not connected to his mind; that, in fact, his mind may be absent and his language has nothing to do with reasoning. I realize Morven is a parrot, some sort of tape recorder, or robot. But where did he learn English? I can only speculate. Perhaps it was passed onto him from his ancestors who, at one time, had their language and thought connected. Through evolution, Morven retained the language but lost the mind. I now know that there is no way to reach Morven because his language means nothing. It is a simple verbal exercise, running on hereditary automatic. I give up trying to insult his American psyche because Morven possesses only the American vocabulary but not the sensibility. I am curious to observe Morven's lifting process and I begin looking around Trella Park for a large, heavy object. I see nothing but an abundance of trees and small stones. But Morven soon takes the trouble from me. He walks to the tree I had been hiding behind and uproots it with apparent ease. He begins gnawing the roots and when he finishes, tosses the tree aside and uproots another. Since his hands are useless, he grabs the tree around the trunk, pulls it to his chest and with one quick jerk, the ground shakes and the tree pulls up. Using his forearms, he hoists the tree up so the roots are at his mouth. He, of course, does this lying on his back. I note that, so far, Morven seems a vegetarian and is perhaps descended from some dinosaur. Is that his weakness? Does his taste for roots suggest his complex of feeling toward his ancestors? Does he want to, at once, destroy and consume them? I decide to test my theory.

It is no use, speech does not touch him.

I notice that Morven remains in or near the center of the park and I try to move him to the edges. I shake a tree to call his attention, I waive the branches suggesting its roots' tastiness. I have chosen the tree most near the sidewalk. Morven drags over but simply consumes the roots in his usual fashion. I decide it isn't geography he values. I recall my introduction, remember that saying my name in a loud tone at close range caused his arm to swell slightly and liquid to come from his mouth. My voice was not enough to cause a fatal reaction but perhaps another's voice would. My quoting another person would probably not be more powerful but less. Apparently, his reaction has to do with the voice and the speaker. It is not powerful to use one without the other, that is, it causes no reaction for me to use my voice to repeat others' words. But, worse, my voice and my words caused only a slight spit and swell. Who, for example, could cause his arm to swell to explosive size and who could cause him to spit so much liquid that he would dehydrate? Perhaps one of his own kind or an image of himself? It seems to me, his destruction needs to involve the ants somehow but in a more powerful stance. Perhaps the answer lie in the notion of will. From what I've read, Morven has always been the passive, that is, the ants have always been thrown onto him. He has never, to my knowledge, found the ants of his free will and through curiosity, killed himself. I walk over to an uprooted tree, pull some of the roots loose and lay them around the ant jar as appetizers. Morven drags over and watches the ants fight. Using his forearms, he crushes the glass and the ants escape onto his back. They bite the bottom of his feet and Morven swells. He begins muttering incoherently and falls to sleep. I now, if my research is correct, have three days until Morven will resume his normal shape. I had first thought that the number of ants could increase his pain and perhaps prove fatal but I now see that fifteen ants cause the same reaction as one. After three days, Morven is as he was, excepting a slight increase in appetite. (Upon waking, he immediately uprooted five trees and ate the roots in great haste.) Should I try my hand on his back again? I can't, I'm afraid he will suck me into him and blister me all over. I have not tried the sensitivity of his bristled hair yet, perhaps I can discover something there. As far as I can tell, I have but three more possibilities: his hair, his face and his hands. I try to work on his face first. Since it is such a perfect circle, I hold up my square notebook and hope the contrast hurts him. He makes a face of displeasure but does not seem to feel pain. Apparently he has grown used to square objects in the park. The lay-out of the grass is itself square, outlined by the sidewalks. I observe his face closely to sense any other possibilities but all other aspects seem almost human. His abundance of flesh and weight is only natural, given his circumstance of diet. Since his hair grows in so odd a position, perhaps it is position he cannot control. I move from my upright position and stand on my head, resting my elbows on my knees. I remember Morven's mistaken value of my knees and when seeing something resting on them, he pulls closer to me. He moves himself around and seems to be trying to touch my knees with one of his feet. He seems more pleased and calm by this position than hurt, he seems attracted. He burrows himself under my uplifted body and I cringe with fear when I notice his mouth begins to open. I suspect he senses me treelike in this position and I stand up immediately. I try one more variation, this time lying on my side. This position has the same effect on Morven as music: he rolls over to his stomach. I resolve my theory: it isn't position he falls into. Position will not cause his death. I try to gesture to the bristled quality of his hair by holding both my hands out, my fingers stiff as bristles. This causes his hair to grow one full inch but again, seems to bring him pleasure, not death. I become fatigued at the versatility of Morven and am near frustration-break. I tell myself, There must be a way. There has got to be a way. There is no monster I can't kill. If I observe close enough, there is no monster I can't kill. I retreat behind a tree in an effort to organize. I inspect my hand to see if the blister has reappeared but it has not. I have only one hope left: his hands. I am discouraged at the narrowness of my choices. I don't like to find myself in such desperate straits. Morven does not seem to suffer from the uselessness of his hands. His arms overcompensate and, in fact, serve his needs completely. How can I hurt and cause death to a monster by attacking a part of him he doesn't need or even value? I gain heart. Perhaps his apparent aloofness signals his real need. Perhaps the death of his hands has caused him such great pain in the past that he has buried the memory of them forever. Perhaps his ignorance of them hides his love for them, his utter dependence on them and his ultimate fear of loss. I have only my pencil and notebook with me now but my pencil will do. It is a small object, difficult to hold and delicate. The pencil is precisely the kind of instrument Morven cannot grasp. I take my pencil and put it first near his small ear. He hears something in it and screams the first sound I have heard him scream. It is a primordial sound, Morven's pre-birth, conceptual sound. He screams the sound of the human sperm fertilizing the human egg. A sound encased in water, muted, in the dark. With this scream, water is vomited from his mouth, ears and arms. The skin of his arms opens up and water pours from his insides. At last, lying in the sun, Morven is on his way to rapid dehydration. I see now suction tenacles growing from his face and he intends to replish his liquid by drinking my blood. I see Morven's ancestry is not dinosaur but vampire. Using a branch I roll the pencil away from his ear and push it into his hand. As the painted wood touches his small palm, he screams a second scream and begins drying. The puddles around him instantly vaporate and his form begins to dry-up. Within minutes he is a thin trunk, a mere sickly tree in the middle of winter. His roots are the last to go.

Sef suffers the frustrating disease of uprightness, that is, not in the moral but in the actual sense: Sef is unable to lie down. He wanders continually, very slowly by now, but I suspect, in his younger years, he was quick. I cannot determine what effect the wandering has had on his general stature but I suspect it has been both healthful and painful. Sef has several growths on the outside of his body, their origins undetermined. In a sense, he is being eaten from the outside-in by living organisms that have grown from the inside-out. The growths themselves do not seem to itch or burn but do continue their expansion. It is hard to imagine, or remember, that Sef's skin was, at one time, rather smoothe, given the usual blemishes. At one time, his skin resembled a woman who has been protected from the sun: white, smoothe, thin. But now, he is wholly disgusting, violently unappetizing. Of all the monsters I have met, Sef has grown the farthest away from his original birth. His being is now mostly a reaction to the growth, his first feelings and personality deeply buried under the necessity of living with it. It is no surprise, therefore, that at any hour of any day Sef can be seen talking to himself in general, addressing his growth in particular. Even though Sef does not speak human language, his voice tones suggest he has given nicknames to each growth and, in fact, seems tenderly attached to them. His voice, which is spoken from his chest, is full of hissing and popping sounds so that when he speaks, one feels near a fire. I've yet to determine his body heat but I suspect it is cold. He has no visible mouth on his chest, the sounds seem to come through him as through a speaker box. I suspect Sef's decline will become fatal when the growths cover his chest and he can no longer give love and affection to his diseased friends. I set out immediately to discover some way of speeding up the growth process. As always, I must observe him closely to get a sense of his life. He is now aimlessly wandering around a tree, not touching anything, silent. Because of his endless motion, his diet is, of course, restricted. He grabs whatever comes by: insects, birds or perhaps, myself. I must keep my distance. As I have mentioned, he is quite slow at this stage of life and not given to chasing. If a bird flies by and Sef reaches but misses, he will not pursue the task but instead try again later. He must sense, therefore, a certain abundance.

To speed up the growth process, I must speed up Sef's pace. I must also discover what brings him pain. Surely the steady pace is a comfort, some stabilizing force. And the growths themselves must be made more violent. I cannot afford to let him live with his growths. As I cannot live with monsters, he must not be allowed to live with his growths. He has now changed trees but not pace. He catches an easy lunch, a butterfly. Some days he must eat all day long, otherwise, how could one small butterfly sustain him? He is not a giant by any means but is, none the less, over eight feet tall. Everything about him is a bit bigger than human but not drastically so. I'm quite sure, given his resistance to chasing, that he will eat both vegetable and animal and although he couldn't eat me entirely in one sitting, he could carry me around for a couple days, eating on me here and there. I shuffle my feet to attract him. He comes over to the bush I'm in and begins circling. Perhaps he is descended from the hawk. No sooner do I speculate when I notice a few feathers on the backs of his arms. Can he fly? I see a spider by my feet, pick it up and hoist it into the air. Sef grabs it. I need something heavier. I pick up a small stone and throw it straight up. Yes! Sef can fly! Why doesn't he fly more often? Why does he content himself with meager chance prey? I try once more, this time throwing the stone at an angle, toward the edge of the park. Again, Sef flies up but I notice he seems restricted in his flight. He is unable to fly toward or away but instead flies like a helicopter on a string. He can only go up. When I tossed the spider, Sef grabbed it quickly and I sensed his keen sight. But now, two possibilities present themselves: (one) Sef's sight is not as keen as I suspected because he can't tell the difference between living and unliving objects, edible objects and non-edible objects, or, (two) Seth not only eats vegetable and animal, but eats mineral as well. Perhaps the eating of mineral has caused his odd growths. I test his appetite one more time by tossing another stone. But with this toss, Sef displays a peculiar ability. His feet remain wandering around the bush while his feathered arms, without leaving his voice-chest, extend themselves high into the air and retrieve the stone. Immediately, I see the disadvantage of this action. Sef's arms remain in the air, grasping the stone, but he cannot bring the stone back down to his mouth. In this position, Sef is able to catch but unable to make use of it. This frustrates him as I see his feet begin to shake as they move and he finally must drop the stone. The stone, meanwhile, has turned into one of the growths on his body. It falls onto him, on his chest, bringing him closer to suffocation. I realize Sef's plight and weakness: he is suffering the disease of impracticality, being unable to make use of his desires. And the disease will prove fatal because the stones do not return neutral, they return harmful. Only when the stone-growth settles in the fertility of his chest do his arms return to their original, more useful, position. Sef's victimization touches my heart but I do not forget his immediate threat to my own life. I can no longer feel honorable compassion toward monsters. The stone test suggests no possible escape for me. If I climb a tree, that is, try to escape him through air, he cannot eat me but can turn me into a growth. On the ground, he can circle me and eat me bit by bit. I must make use of his inability to fly at an angle and avoid his arms at all costs. Because of his arms, it seems safer for me on the ground. I have not seen him able to extend his arms except upward. He seems, when on the ground, only able to wander. I have not been able to get close enough to the growths themselves, perhaps they can be used against him. If he, in fact loves them, as I suspect, then I need only use them to break him. I begin running from tree to tree in an effort to break his pace. But he remains steady. If I could only detach one of the growths, toss it into the air, Sef would grasp it, perhaps the process would reverse itself, the stone would fall into his chest and he would die in one of two ways: (one) by eventual poisoning of the skin, caused by the foreign element or (two) by the very fact of reversal. It seems that Sef is pitifully restricted in direction, that is, his arm is one-directional, his flight is one-directional. It is when Sef aspires to the two-directional, when he attempts to first reach up and then down, he suffers. It is not only reversal he cannot tolerate, it is multi-direction. I gather several stones then toss them into the air. Sef grabs one, lets it fall, the growth process begins but the others don't come down at all! In fact, the number of stones caused one growth to grow but, in addition, caused one to disappear. No good. If I continue that process, Sef will remain as he is. What I must do is invert the growths. They must be made to grow inward, overtake his circulation, clog the works. But how? Maybe I have overlooked something, there must be a simple solution. But first, before I can find the simple solution, I must summarize and simplify the problem: Sef is (1) a slow and steady wanderer (2) has outside, expanding growths (3) capable of tenderness toward growths (4) has voice on chest (5) body heat, unknown (6) reactions to growths, including sense of abundance (7) has feathers (8) capable of flying only straight up (9) capable of arm extension but only when on ground, only up (10) capable of frustration, manifested as feet shaking, caused by inability to make use of desired object.

I have failed to determine his body heat and must do so rapidly. I have seen the reaction to stone and small insect. I have not seen his reaction to vegetable or plant. Perhaps the process of plant growth is intolerable to him. In general, Sef seems to prefer moving objects, that is, objects moving prior to their stasis: the thrown stone or the landed butterfly. Is it stasis he can't consume? My first speculation on direction, seems to me now, inadequate. I must strike Sef in an area he has nothing of. In the directional, he has minimal skill. But in the static, he is helpless. Is this why he must consume stones? Does he want the world free of stones? In Trella park, there are several stones remaining immobile and undisturbed. The trick will be to bring Sef to them somehow since my bringing the stones to Sef would induce mobility. How then am I to bring Sef to the static and from there, force an interaction between the active and the static? With Sef's sense of abundance, he is not likely to push for an interaction. He is more likely to simply pass over the statis, wander around elsewhere. I have already discovered there is no use in quantity. To Sef, one stone has, more or less, the same quality as several. I must choose one stone, observe it closely, and determine my plan. In Trella Park, all the stones are about the same so I choose one at random, one that happens to have survived the tosses. It is slightly smoothed, slightly rounded, nothing distinguished about it. A common rock. Some mixture of greys, whites, blacks. In keeping with Sef's tenderness, I name my stone Touftch and mutter a few endearing remarks at it. The stone remains the stone. I leave it lying still. I am confident that the answer to Sef's death lie in the relationship between stone, growth, and the variable X. I now name the variable X: heat. Sef's death lies between stone, growth, and heat. I look around me, around the park, searching for the answer. What is it that lies between stone, growth and heat? I look down to my own feet. A second stone is near my left foot, a stone I hadn't seen. The puzzle distresses me, causes the back of my head to ache. I lie down to rest between stones. The grass of Trella Park is grown around me and the sun is above me. Is it me? No, that's silly. I knew that when I first saw him, I knew I would be the one killing him, that's not what I'm after, it's something else. Besides, I have no weapons, my pencil and notebook long gone. I couldn't bare to stab him with a sword even if I had one. Who knows how contagious those horrible sores are? Who knows what would happen to my sword? I stand firm in my riddle. I am sure his death lies between stone, growth and heat. Sef is circling around me now but I don't rise, I lie still, I still have time. He seems more curious than hungry but I know this won't last long. Without warning, Sef extends his arm and grasps an infected owl. His feet shake as before, the frustration! The owl falls onto his chest, becomes a growth, as the stones had become growths, but the owl growth remains half-formed, uglier than the rest, oozing, more alive. Perhaps Sef will cause his own death, a suicide of greed, impatience. Perhaps his sense and faith in the abundance of prey is failing! Perhaps he'll die from the response to his loss of faith! Sef's ability of reaction has been established from the first. His sense of original being long buried, Perhaps if the nature of his growths change, the nature of his reactions will change. If the nature of his growths become malignant, the nature of his reactions will become malignant. Again, I watch Sef reach into the sky and grasp a hummingbird. The resutant growth from the hummingbird is even more ugly, bigger, bloody. Is it some sort of declining process that causes the growths to become worse each time? Has something gone awry in his make-up? Or are the birds themselves, the types of birds, dictating the response? Why has the hummingbird caused so ugly a reaction, why worse than the infected owl? It must be the hummingbird's habit of flight-- a habit similar to Sef's, the upward motion, the helicopter-like hovering. Is it possible that the worst growths will come from Sef's grasping things most like himself? He no longer bothers to bring his arm down in retreat but is holding it up there as a net, grasping, catching whatever comes by. It begins to rain but has no effect on him. The water does not evaporate on him. His body heat is cold, as I first expected. Soon his entire body begins to shake as his feet shook earlier and I sense he is trying to lift off the ground entirely. He seems to want to join his extended arm, high in the air but cannot. The rain slows to a drizzle. The sun returns and a sharp-colored rainbow grows in the sky. The reds are deep, the greens and blues blinding. What has he done? Is the sky infected? I feel a heat from the sky, not the sun heat, a more direct, burning heat. The Park temperature rises. I shield my eyes as best I can and try to get a look at the odd rainbow. The colors are all there, much brighter, but there nonetheless. I count them and see three additional ones: some mixture of greys, whites and blacks, the rock colors, the toufch colors, burning in the sky, the sky itself threatening to become stone! Sef is trying to turn the world to stone, the sky, the park. But his arm begins failing him. It does not return to his body. He seems too weak to retrieve it and he dies in the awkward stance of a power unable to direct the form of the world.

Jymuti has two eyes on one side of her head. One eye is approximately two inches above the other. The other side of her head is humanlike, that is, possessing one ear partially covered by hair. Her front face has an ordinary nose and mouth. Only her eyes are displaced. Her resting position is standing upright and it is in this position that I first see her. Judging by the duration of her resting period (3-5 minutes) I assume that only her eyes require rest while the rest of her body remains active. She does not close her eyes to rest but rather opens them, stretches them. The elastic texture of the side of her head gives way and, during rest, the entire side of her head is eye. Perhaps the intensity of the rest makes up for the short rest period, that is, the intensity makes up for the necessity of time. The enlargement of the eyes, the increase of surface area--these allow for greater reception by letting the rest fall in large amounts. When the eyes have their fill of rest, they return to their normal size but remain, at all times, on the side of her head. Jymuti seems a fairly stable creature, that is, her parts seem confined to her body. However, I must not be too quick to summarize. I see her now, active, lying on the grass, eyes in odd position but normal proportion. Her ears are in human position but given her side-eyes, one of the ears falls in between the eyes while the other ear is alone, amongst the hair. I've yet to observe her activities but suspect one of two things: (one), she is severly restricted because of her horizontal position or (two) she is able to change form somehow, produce various additional parts that will be used in defense. If she has no inhuman, superhuman attributes, she will surely fall prey to the first ground-monster that comes along. I see no spectacular means of locomotion. Her legs seem human, even shapely. Her arms, likewise, are human sized and seem to function as mine do. I've yet to hear her talk or watch her eating patterns. I am also puzzled by my research. Previous scholars have suggested Jymuti's life-span is a mere 36 hours. If that is so, I've not much time to kill her and I would feel a horrible failure if she were to die of natural causes. I must set about my task immediately. I must move closer for a better look.

Jymuti clears a section of grass and begins drawing pictures in the dirt with a small stick--a picture of a monster much like herself, perhaps her mother or father. She brings the stick to her stomach every few minutes as if her belly is an inkwell. When she finishes the drawing, her breaths are short and awkward. She begins again. This time she draws a square first, showing her need to outline, but she quickly abandons the drawing, stands up and rests. She seems to be finished with the artistic part of her life. Given the short life-span, the minutes she spent drawing is, in human terms, approximately twenty years. Suddenly, I sense a peculiar function of her eyes. She poses sideways, astraddle the pictures, and her eyes fall to her pelvic area, each eye occupying a hip. She views the pictures from that position (in our terms, about two years.) The eyes then move to her upper arm for, again, our time, two more years. I follow this eye pattern for several hours (years.) Jymuti's eye pattern is as follows: (1) pelvic (2) upper arm (3) hand-palm (4) ankle (5) neck (6) chest (7) belly (8) return to side-head. She then stands away from the drawings and rests.

Her next activity resembles the human oddity of hair-curling. She takes a strand of hair and twists it in a knot. The hair remains knotted on its own. She then takes several long vines, ties them together and, using two sticks, begins a process similar to knitting. I sense a gentleness in her. I begin to question her identity as monster when she suddenly expands, like a huge piece of dough or a balloon, and before I can realize what's happened, I find myself trapped inside! I believe she's become one big belly! I feel around the walls that are sticky and elastic. The area seems as large as Trella Park and the smell of the air is similar to the park air. I am walking on several bones and can see down inside her legs. I see her veins and yellow blood. I see no heart. I won't suffocate here, there is no shortage of air. I could starve or die of thirst. The temperature is about 80 degrees, the sound is restful, in fact, almost hypnotizing, and I have to fight emphatic drowsiness. I sense the danger of sleeping here, a sure Rip Van Winkle sleep, a too-long sleep. I must get out! How did Jonah do it? Pinnochio? Captain Nemo? Is she descended from the whale? I remember her eyes, that odd but seemingly harmless roving, where are they now? Sitting on top of this bloated mass? I look around the walls but see nothing save elastic. At my feet, bones and the leg-pits. That's where I must go, down the leg, into the dark, holding onto the muscles. I lower myself with the chronic fear of disappearing forever. Is there no one else down here? I scream for anyone, anyone, mythic or real. No one. The leg gets thinner and thinner and near the ankle, I touch both sides and barely squeeze through. Then, the opening. I see it. Near the ankle. I peer out, My God! The eyes! That's where they are, on the ankle, peering in. The ankles begin contracting and my breath is being squeezed out of me. I force the walls back and try to squeeze myself down into the foot. Finally, down in the foot, another opening, very small, I peer out. No one is looking in, I can see Trella Park directly outside below. I must find a way to force the opening,

My finger fits through the hole. It feels stiff and brittle and the outside of the hole cracks and sounds like walking on broken leaves. Jymuti moves and I crouch in fear of being located. Can she turn herself inside out and find me? And if she did, what would she do? Tear me apart then knit me back together? Use my blood to paint with? Twist my spine and use it as decor for her head? What's the purpose of this swelling? Why does she bother if she's not going to use gastric juices to weaken, destroy and digest me? Why does she want me in here? She rolls on her back and I fall, banging the back of my head on a bone. Unconscious.

I awake in the same prediciment as before. Again I force my finger through the hole to test its expansion. It contracts-- what? Jymuti seems to be sticking something in from the outside, a small blade of grass? Is she trying to tickle, tease me? Is she an ogre?

I am overcome with a sense of the useless. But I notice, simultaneously, a strange mist gathering above the ankle-- ocean blue in color, smelling of salt, seeming, in fact, wholly marine. But the mist disappears as quickly as it appeared and again I stand baffled by Jymuti's nonsensical, nonproductive, pointless activities. Why does she bother to produce an ocean mist that has no purpose? It simply appears, then, disappears. What a fool she is! She will doddle her life away with all these trite bodily functions! Again, in the same position, above the ankle, a human face appears, this time, a fanged male. At first, I am frightened but as I watch it disappear, I know the area above her ankle is like the movie screens they used to have.

Does she simply reproduce what she's seen? Or are these images hers? After the fang, an image of an accordian appears and, for the first time since I was swallowed, surrounded, enveloped, I hear a sound other than circulation. Then, an image of a doorway appears. I scream curses at her--Have you no order you imbecile! Idiot! Why bother with these silly images, they mean nothing! Teach nothing! Do nothing! Do you expect me to sit through all this, all in the name of some perversity, some entertainment? Two thoughts occur to me through my disgust: (one), I must force myself to respect her because only through respect will I be able to see her clearly enough to destroy her and (two), I must be determined and faithful to my belief in pattern. I must find the pattern to these images even though they seem banal and random. They must tell something about her nature. They must help me first escape then destroy. I am also noticing the tendency to think in pairs while inside this bloat and I must guard against any attempt Jymuti might make of either splitting me in half or making me twin. There is an abundance of dual thinking in this environment and I sense the fatality and narrowness. I must not forget the simple fact of her identity: monster.

With the hole entirely closed, I sense a rocking, as if on a ship in some ocean. Another Jymutian illusion. Trella Park has no water, no ocean and Jymuti is no ship. I wait it out, try to recall the images, the order: the mist, the fang, the accordian, the doorway. Is it possible that, through the images, she has shown me the only possible escape? Shown me, not through tenderness but through the simple biological phenomena of image creation? The mist, the fang, the accordian, the doorway -- are these pairs? Yes, the mist is a natural enough environment for fanged creatures, every child knows as much. But the accordian and the doorway? Perhaps, but pairs in what? Sound? Taste? Sight? Yes, that's it, pairs in sight: the arch. The arch of the open accordian and the arch of the doorway.

My escape has to do with environment and arch. I begin looking. Squeeze up through the leg, back to the belly area. How is it she is a bloated mass but still retains human form? How is she able to bloat and all the while, remain legged? My escape is too desperate now, I can't play with the trivial, perhaps the leg-pit was not leg at all, the area I called ankle, not ankle at all. I'll never know, I only want out! I squeeze from the belly area to the neck, the head, where is the body arch? I ponder my direction, look for the birth canal, yes, an arch of sorts. I begin to walk down, time slows, slows, I am getting nowhere, each step leads no closer, what has she done? I will never get there walking. I am walking in place, growing tired, moving in no direction. The environment-- is there something I missed? Is there something here, some secret I haven't seen? I feel the temperature, a sure 80 degrees, crisp air. Nothing. I sit in despair, afraid her eyes may appear at any second. In time, in just a couple hours, she will die her natural death but I must get out! I don't want to die with her! I prop myself up against a wall, begin crying, begin dying the death of a failure and coward. One hour left. Despair.

I hear a clicking noise. I try to locate it. Arm? Head? No. Belly. She must be tapping her belly with a stick. She must be drawing. Why does this meaningless creature continue her meaningless gestures? I tap back, pound the walls as hard as I can with both fists. Scream Let me out! Nothing. The sporatic tapping goes on. I hear her short and awkward breaths as before and can imagine her straddling. I wonder what picture she has drawn this time. I am slightly comforted by the notion of her habit, fairly predictable. The second time around. I have seen her entire pattern. But why does she remain in the bloated stance? I review her activities in my mind: drawing, straddling, roving eyes, curling, knitting. At once, my escape becomes apparent. I sense her particular sensibility: entwining. Bringing together. This is her necessity. Her undoing will come when she can no longer entwine. I begin my escape.

I walk to the left belly wall, scratch, kick, beat and scream. I don't know if she hears me. I walk to the front belly wall, as close as I can get to the place she taps the stick. I beat there, scream and kick. Then, I do the same thing on the right wall. That will suffice. I want her to feel three presences, disjointed, refusing to entwine. Three alienations. Can she hear me? Perhaps. I am thrown flying as she stands up in restful position. A hole opens near the rib cage and the eyes peer in at me. They search the insides, looking for the source of the other two sounds. I take my shoe off and throw it against the far wall. With the sound, her eyes seem full of horror and The Fang image is manifested again but this time in the belly area, displaced, the face utterly disproportionate, nearly a scribble. Her powers are failing! I quickly toss my other shoe against an an opposite wall. The doorway and accordian, both surrounded by mist, are superimposed in confusion, their arch's flattened. The actual practice of drawing loses its reality as she turns it inside herself, into an image, and I stand watching an image of the activity she once lived. The practices of knitting and curling lose their actuality as well and are projected as foggy shadows. My heart is touched as I watch the image of Jymuti fumble in frustration as she tries to knot and knit with no clear picture of her hands. Within seconds, the bloated mass itself is an image, her entire form an image with only a thin skin holding it all in. Finally, as the skin itself attempts image, it flashes, then dies of exposure to the air of Trella Park. I stand free, looking at the park and pronounce Jymuti a double death. She was first turned from monster to image but since there was no monster to contain the image, the image itself died. Jymuit is dead because of her inability to understand the reality of alienation. Because she could not accept the inevitable failure to entwine, she lost both the illusion and the actuality.

The End

Brain Trust

CHAPTER ONE

At Home

Elijah lay on his back in bed. His left arm was resting on his forehead. His eyes were closed. He was crying. The tears made partial circles as they fell across his cheeks. They ran down behind his ears to his neck and then onto his pillowcase. He lay crying a long time. It was morning.

After awhile, while still in bed, he reached over and got a book from the top of his dresser. He started reading. He read through tears. He read for a long time.

He sat up. The tears dropped from his eyes onto the open book but he kept reading anyway. The book had many tears on it. He stayed in bed. He cried and read for a long time. Soon he placed the book back on the top of the dresser and lay back down again. He placed his left arm across his forehead like before and continued crying.

The day soon ended and it became night.

It was in the winter and the day outside was very cold. He thought about going to a store but he didn't. He just stayed in bed crying.

Some time in the night Elijah turned on his left side for awhile and slept.

The next morning he awoke and tears filled his eyes again.

He stayed in bed and cried. He pulled the blanket up to the top of his neck and went back to sleep.

CHAPTER TWO

Professor Elijah Torahfeld In His Office and Beyond

Professor Elijah Torahfeld was in his office on Monday morning. He was sitting at his academic desk. His academic desk was very different from his desk at home. He was writing.

His university-based office was on the second floor of the English Department.

Some time ago, he had been asked, along with three other professors, to lecture at the Jewish Theological Seminary of America in the fall. He was writing an acceptance to the invitation.

After folding the sheet of stationary in thirds, he inserted the acceptance into the envelope and sealed it.

He opened his journal. Turning past yesterday's journal writing without reading it, he placed his pen at the top of the clean page.

Before beginning to write, he looked at the spines of some of the books that were neatly arranged on his desk.

He wrote in his journal.

Then, after finishing his journal writing, he gently closed his journal. He left the journal and pen on his desk.

The department was sponsoring a guest writer. He was supposed to arrive some time in the afternoon. In the evening he would be reading from his work-in-progress. All the professors were to meet him in the department library in the afternoon.

Professor Torahfeld planned on attending.

He read a novel until the afternoon. The meeting in the library began.

Professor Torahfeld got up from his desk. He gathered his pens, notebook, coat and thoughts. He looked around his office to make sure he hadn't forgotten anything. He straightened all the things on his desk. Happy that things seemed in order, he closed his office door and locked it. He locked his door out of a respect for form, not physcial necessity. The people in the adjoining offices were regularly comforted by his continuity. His familiar, measured steps could be heard as he walked into the library.

Some of the professors were already seated, busily scribbling on their pads. No one addressed him.

Professor Torahfeld took a seat in a middle chair at the oak conference table with his back to a wall of literary journals. This was a quizzical position for him because no one read nor loved literary journals more.

Professor Torahfeld began scribbling on a pad like all the other professors, mostly because it seemed the going thing to do. There were about 20 well-schooled professors at the table.

It could have been called a meeting of the minds except that they did not speak to each other. Any meeting of the minds would have had to have been purely telepathic.

Professor Torahfeld's incessant scribbling started to cohere into a essay, even though it was temporarily somewhat formless.

As the professors were busy with their own thoughts, the visiting writer walked quietly in and took a seat.

CHAPTER THREE

Professor Torahfeld Attends A Reading

After dinner, Professor Torahfeld got ready to go to the university for the reading. He placed his dinner dishes in the dishwasher and cleaned the top of his dining room table. Then, he placed the dining room chair with the table where it belonged.

He brought his journal with him to the reading. That was not unusual. He had taken his journal with him everwhere for years.

He was soon in front of the auditorium where the reading was to take place.

He walked to the auditorium doors, opened the door and entered.

For some reason, some of the female ushers recognized him.

"Good evening Professor Torahfeld," the usher said.

"Good evening Professor Torahfeld," another usher said.

Professor Torahfeld generously supplied good evenings all around wherever they seemed needed.

When he was in his typically uncomfortable seat, 121,648E, he opened his journal and jotted down a few notes from his reading of the novel earlier in the day.

The guest writer soon appeared on the stage wearing a suit of a God-awful color. He proceeded to give a reading to match.

Professor Torahfeld's sincere wish was that the very rough draft really was a work-in-much-need-of-progress. In fact, it seemed to him as if it had barely begun. If the guest writer thought of it as anywhere more than one-eighth complete, then it was a futile effort. It was one of the worst pieces of writing he had ever heard and that was saying something because he had spent 2 semesters trying to teach people that could only be described as older versions of the type of children that Agnes Grey had to contend with and suffer through. His young teaching years were a nightmare filled with nudniks and tiresome little clods.

He could not discern precisely what the problem was. There seemed to be no major problems. The guest writer did not appear to be overtly stupid, drunk or recently traumatized. Perhaps he had had bad teachers.

Professor Torahfeld vaguely thought for a few moments if it was possible to get an earache just from something one has heard.

At any rate, it was soon ended and no one was more thankful and relived than Professor Torahfeld. The writing had actually hurt his ears.

After shaking a few hands that belonged to people he wasn't sure he ever knew, he reasoned that such occasions required these kinds of seemingly meaningless gestures. Then, without wanting to seem impolite, he left as quickly as he could.

Once he got home, he placed his journal and pen on the dining room table and went to bed. He wanted to entirely forget about it.

CHAPTER FOUR

Fourteen Books To Read

Professor Torahfeld went to the university bookstore before walking to his office.

There weren't too many people there. He thought that was good because it meant it would be peaceful and quiet. It seemed to Professor Torahfeld that there weren't very many peaceful, quiet places anymore. He had recently said something about that to Professor Mirthful, a professor in the imbriferology department, but Professor Mirthful, ever the antithesis of his name, just told him it was ill-adapted nonsense, out of keeping with the tasks of the day. He didn't want to hear anymore about it.

This distressing retort sent Professor Torahfeld into a revery about how people are often unlike their names. He thought Professor Mirthful's name should probably have been Professor Crabcake. However, life being as it is, with wonders never ceasing and all of that, his thoughts soon changed course.

The bookstore was particularly enheartening this morning. He didn't know why. But not being one to question where there is nothing to be gained by it, he accepted and answered each cheerful Hello and Good Morning that was tossed his way. Who was he to resent anyone else's happiness?

djioinsijioingjio   gggggddopoiioijijioijdfhfhf

mpom   shoingngn   oioio½½½p½p½p;½ kk

nngighgngnggjjg

           lkdjkjlkjklkjkeiri   jjj

nnnniioiinioi   nnnnnnnnnnnasdasdsdjkioji

jiojioj   ddddjioij   iojijoij ;;

aaaaaaaaaaa   dopopok okop kkodkf mkjfodkk

           ioioioii99   jj   jjl;l;l;   llll

qweqweqwewewpopopklkl   hghghdfdfsggsjjioi

Editor's Note

Printing Machine Problems

After making his way to a section he found interesting, and being very adept, after years of practice, at reading book titles sideways, he began quickly scanning the shelves relevant to his interest.

Professor Torahfeld typically vocalized his thoughts to himself while reading. Ah, hmmmm, oh, I don't know, possibly, I suppose, were the things that could be heard on the aisles nearby. Professor Torahfeld had become somewhat of a laughing stock among the students for this vocal practice. He tried to think of which books he would like to have in his home to read at his leisure.

After choosing fourteen, he walked to the cashier and it was soon a done deal.

Meanwhile, the books would have to have a temporary home in his department office until the end of the day when he could include them in his library.

Professor Torahfeld walked up the department stairs. The people already there heard the familiar footsteps. After saying his usual distance, formal Hello to whomever happend to be in his trajectory, he unlocked his office door and entered.

He placed his 14 new books on his desk, closed his door and locked it. He went back downstairs out of the department building.

As he walked towards his classroom where he was to teach his afternoon class, he noticed Professor Gladden sitting near the physical education building. Amazing as it seems, Professor Gladden was 847 years old.

Professor Torahfeld approached Professor Gladden.

Good day, Hello, and all of that followed.

After several moments of decorative silence, and since no one had died and therefore no formal silent moments were required, Professor Torahfeld asked Professor Gladden how he had been.

To this politeness Professor Gladden remained far afield.

After a few moments, Professor Gladden spoke. It sounded like someone that hasn't spoken in years.

"I wrote a perfectly fine letter to the editor," he said. "I sent it to the editorial page editor, oh, some weeks ago and then today, this morning in fact, I received a strange reply. It seems the editor threw away my editorial without even reading it."

In brief, it seems the editor had been in no mood that day to read anyone's things. The reason was that LQLMCT, the editor's wife of nine years, had left him. She had changed her name to the L conglomeration one night after he made fun of her Estee Lauder face creams, forbade her to go parasailing and called her a refusenik. Her complaints against him were ruefully and regrettably numerous. She accused him of breaking her LLadro collectible actually spilling coffee on her favorite coffee table book she screamed at him that that is not what coffee table book actually means for buying way too many aerosol cans on August 10 1993 she said he date raped her she said he was a fogey and an egg head that he made fun of the part of her will that says that she wants the use of cryonics and other things

Professor Torahfeld, a seasoned and durable sufferer of compassion fatigue, felt more sorry for the editor than he did for Professor Gladden. He, therefore, didn't know what to say.

After a few more decorative silences, Professor Gladden finally summed up his feelings.

"It's enough to make me live differently than my name implies," he said.

Professor Torahfeld said Good bye, wished his well, and, in short, supplied all the decorum the situation seemed to require. Then, he headed off towards the familiar classroom door.

He couldn't have asked for a more beautiful day. It was just like one of Goncharova's bright paintings.

CHAPTER FIVE

Similarity

Professor Torahfeld looked around at the furnishings in his living room. He remembered John Fathom, an old college acquaintance that ended up working in a furniture store. Like many people, John Fathom had crowded into his life somehow and had appeared here and there at times, now and then. Three of the pieces in his living room were handmade by Brainy Farsight, a craftsman he had met at a poetry reading near Columbia University many years ago. Even though the forgotten bard had typically faded into oblivion years ago, and is now in poetry heaven where the meter flows freely, he had provided Elijah the opportunity for a conversation with the craftsman. The poetic impulse-turned-occurrence spawned a working relationship that produced three pieces of furniture.

His coffee table was made of glass and steel. He liked it because it was made from those materials. He preferred materials of a cold temperament, far from nature's warmness or soft shapes. He himself was not of this temperament. He liked the simple and smooth look of things. All the machines of the workaday world did not bother him. He liked their whirling sounds and saw them all as somewhat comical human imitations.

Professor Torahfeld walked to the living room window. Opening the gold, thickly lined drapes, he looked out across the field opposite. He remembered that he had purchased a new journal for writing his thoughts.

He returned to the interior of the living room. He began crying. The fits of crying were a part of him, a part of his life. There was something basic in him that needed these tears. He cried regularly.

When his tears subsided, he lay on his left side thinking. He had lost the book he had been reading. He lost books from time to time. Where was it? Had he mislaid it at Nibblewit's, a coffee shop a few miles from the university? He had made it up to 243, chapter 19. Well, that's the way it was. Perhaps he could begin one of the 14 recently purchased novels. Where had he placed them anyway? Oh yes. In the bookshelf, near the hallway, near the ancestral cabinet, near some of America's great poetry. Professor Torahfeld dried his eyes with soft tissue and walked toward his bookshelf.

The ancestral cabinet, which he passed by several times each day, had been given him by his grandfather who had inherited it from his grandfather. Professor Torahfeld had never known quite what to do with it or how to approach it suitably. Therefore, he usually hurried past it, conscious of its presence but not knowing how to think of it. He was torn between reverence for its history and anxiety lest he mar it in some way. Perhaps that's how things were. One couldn't really live comfortably with prized possessions. One needed things that would allow breakage, getting rumpled and used. One needed resilient things. After all, one can not feel that one is walking around in a porcelain world.

Professor Torahfeld walked to his bookshelf. Near his books on ships and boats, he found a note he had never seen before. He opened it. It was from his father, now deceased 14 years.

"You know it wasn't much to ask," the note began. "Just to go to the store and buy the rope parrel, fore stay, oar lanyard and ring bolt for the ship I was working on. What, you couldn't find the time? I'm not important enought? What a nudnik son you are. Cretin.

Your deserving but denied
Father"

Ah, yes, Professor Torahfeld thought. He should have run the errand for his father. What he wouldn't give now, just to have his father call him an idiot once more.

He walked to the garage. He brought his father's ship out of a dusty box then, returning indoors, placed it in the center of the coffee table. There it was, just as he had left it. Perhaps he should leave it on the coffee table? Again, torn feelings of reverence and anxiety occurred. He was afraid he might damage it. Should he place it back in the box?

Professor Torahfeld thought he would have to sustain the torn feelings as part and parcel of his life. Maybe that's just the way some things are, he reasoned. Some things are just-- and will remain inherently contradictory and never resolved, unless doing nothing more is a kind of resolution?

After some thought, Professor Torahfeld decided to leave the ship on the table. He thought it could be seen as a kind of sculpture or as a ship in any of Winslow Homer's paintings.

With these thoughts complete, Professor Torahfeld set his mind upon another task.

CHAPTER SIX

A Pirate's Gift

Professor Torahfeld was at his desk in his university office. He was writing in his ever-present journal. Aside from the Hellos to some of the people that worked in and around the office, he said nothing. Sometimes his entire day passed without his speaking.

On this particular day, he was thinking about Professor Carefor. Professor Carefor was esteemed Professor of Plum and Nectarine Trees.

Professor Torahfeld had spoken to him earlier in the week about the 97 plum and nectarine trees that Professor had planted some time ago in his back yard. There was nothing wrong with the trees. It was just that they needed their specialized care. It was that time again.

The conversation lasted a little more than an hour. There had been numerous variations of the same conversation through the years. Professor Torahfeld thought about how he could make the conversation more interesting for both of them. Professor Torahfeld noticed that, at times, during the conversation, Professor Carefor would roll his eyes heavenward and move part of his mouth downward as if to say Egad, here we go again.

Professor Torahfeld employed various strategies for trying to liven things up. Sometimes he used words that no one had ever heard of. However, the effect that had on the conversation became predictable. Professor Carefor would just say "Whatever you think." During a conversation nearly 5 years ago, when the idea had first occurred to Professor Torahfeld, Professor Carefor responded with his "Whatever you think" no less than fifteen times. Professor Torahfeld swiftly saw that this particular idea had limited potential.

He tried asking Professor Carefor's opinion. This idea met with Professor Carefor's asking if Professor Torahfeld felt well because they had gone over the terms several years ago. Professor Carefor thought that something seemed to be affecting Professor Torahfeld's memory.

Professor Torahfeld tried to continue thinking of ways to keep the conversation interesting.

This particular week was the week Professor Carefor was to begin work on the plum and nectarine trees. He was looking forward to returning home to his loved trees. Seeing them well-cared for made his heart soar.

Each day when Mr. Carefor would return, after work, to his inspiriting home, his family was there. He had a wife and 3 children, 2 girls and 1 boy. The children were all happy and well-proportioned. Professor Carefor's 3 children were named Esmeralda, Eulalia and Innocenzio. They each had different personalities, as children do. Their characteristics were evident at an early age. Esmeralda, for instance, was uncommonly yielding in her relations with the other children and was fond of liverwurst. Eulalia was predictive, continually informing people of events that eventually ended up occurring. Innocenzio was easily bruised and seemed to be going around in a continued weakened state of one kind or another.

Mr. Carefor's physical health was good. He was about forty years old. He had been born in Elfwick and had had a healthy start.

In his school, he had been a serious student which had served him well throughout his life. His study habits had been established when he was young and stayed with him his entire life. His life may seem unremarkable, but his steadfastness and unswerving diligence were qualities of character not developed in most people. It was, in fact, his character that was the chief reason for his success, although his intellect was considerable, as well. His wife, a native of nearby Eggs Up, loved him.

When he would work on the plum and nectarine trees, birds of all kinds, shapes and sizes would keep him company. The long-turquoise-beaked Gibbles, native to Intalsia, were his usual company but the long-pink-throated Meccolitlia, with feathers that changed color every other month, were the most abundant. The long-gold-toned Shirkster, known for her distinctive sound made only when walking on the ground, was a frequent visitor as well. At times the Grinning Nibebitt, distinctive, in face, with top of head feathers blue in fall, white in spring, showed up. He would often think of them, as they were near him, and he thought that maybe someday he could learn to talk with them, not through sound, though, through thought.

Professor Carefor's home had once been the subject of a newspaper story because of the orchard he planted. The story had caused only a slight commotion. The only difference that Professor Carefor noticed was that for about two weeks new and never-seen-before cars started driving by their house.

The chldren thought it was great fun, though. They had been told beforehand that a reporter was to be at their house. Basically, they were told to pick up their toys and to stay out of sight.

When the reporter showed up, Eulalia pulled on the bottom of his coat until he leaned to her.

Yes?

She told him that even though the orchard looked fine now, her father had plans to improve it. She said that she could not disclose the investment particulars, however, that she would like it known that her father was actually and in fact worth well over sixteen million because, unbeknowest to people, he had found a buried treasure, basically in a chest from a ship wreck, full of enormous jewels which he uses from time to time whenever he wants to make changes or improvements, as not all changes are improvements, of course, and that, basically, the pirate's treasure will be used in future to enhance the orchard and that what he is looking at now is just small potatoes.

It was printed up next day, somewhat curious to some, including Professor Carefor. He never asked Eulalia the reasons for the statement, but Eulalia saw that it was okay because she thought she could sense that, beneath her father's habitual, stern look, a smile was just waiting to break through. He retained his serious look but Eulalia hadn't missed the small, upturned sides of his mouth and the way he had had to make a effort to keep from laughing. Life was, after all, such serious business to him.

A Spiritual Presence

by

Sharon McPeters

Translated from the Portugese by Y.I. R. Y. Fresco, QY.L

Belfast and Dublin, LTD

2005

Professor Torahfeld thought that he would go to the university library later on in day. He hadn't been for awhile. He liked to be able to freely roam around the library shelves reading bits and pieces as he walked along. At times he would sit in one of the pink library cubicles and read. The cubicles seemed cramped to him. He was used to his more spacious office, but he reveled in the anonymity of being among the students. He had been a good student all those years ago. Isn't a professor a great student first? In his view, the professorship is just the next step after student life.

Before going to the library though, he was going to try to have to behave in an engaged manner at a brief department meeting scheduled for ten o'clock. The department had successfully learned to keep the meetings under 15 minutes, which was nice because everyone knew that no one really wanted to be there. The department's few remaining wind bags had been brought under control some months ago.

The meeting soon ended without consequence, as usual.

Professor Torahfeld bid them Goodbye. An occasional, flourishing "Fare well" could be heard issuing forth from other professors. That seemed out of place to Professor Torahfeld because he'd soon be seeing them at another meeting.

Professor Torahfeld stood outside the library doors for a few minutes admiring the day and the trees.

Then, he entered.

Heading straight for the international literature shelves, he began reading.

Professor Torahfeld was in the library for more than 3 hours. This was not unusual for him.

He read one book longer than usual. He liked the way that it was written and paused for a few moments over some of the quizzical, puzzling words. He did not know their meanings. The words were not new, but they seemed from a different time. He checked the date of copyright. No, it was written recently. What could a modern writer mean by such terms as "sacralize," "Priestess," or, "nontraditional work patterns," for that matter. What was he to think of A precis, historical linguistics, geographic mobility, occupational patterns, occupational attitudes, change agents, myrmidon, mythogenic, intonaco, giornate, or immram?

After he finished reading, he left the library and went home.

As he drove to his house, he saw a formless, cloudlike shape, seemingly floating or hovering above his house.

He watched it for awhile. It changed colors and shapes. The colors and shapes seemed to have endless variations.

At first he thought maybe an artist of some kind had taken it into his head to place a new artwork there. He parked his car in his driveway and hurriedly went to see what it was.

Professor Torahfeld prided himself on knowing what to do when things presented themselves. He thought he was good at thinking on his feet and able to think of solutions on the spur of the moment.

He set his mind to the task.

After several discarded definitions, including a new kind of animal that was part cow, lion, swan, and flamingo, he decided that it was a spiritual presence of some kind. He did not know what kind.

He approached closer, a step at a time.

The spiritual presence moved, up, back, and away from him, then, disappeared into the sky.

Professor Torahfeld went to write at his desk. He sat at his desk by the window and wrote in his journal.

He wrote about his day.

As he looked out his window to reflect, he saw old Mr. Enhearten, the man that had lived down the street all these years.

Mr. Enhearten reached to the address on his front walkway and added 97634 to the already 359.

Then, he placed a huge Have A Happy Life sign in his yard, even though the day was no different than any other day.

Mr. Enhearten quietly returned inside his home.

The End

Soliloquey's Life

So the novel begins in the only place I have ever really loved, sunny California.

So much for the setting.

I could have set the novel in other places, but why would I write about places I don't like?

Since it is important for me to love my book, I write about things I love. In other words, I write about things that make me happy.

It makes no sense to write about sad things. I'm no Victor Hugo.

Why have so many people written sad books? Did they sell better in those days? Do readers think that you have to be sad to be a genius?

I don't care a fig. I'm just trying to get by.

You may meet me now and get to know me a little better. (Pleased to meet you. Or, as Tatyana Tolstaya wrote in <u>On the Golden Porch</u>: "How don't you do.") I don't care what other people think.

I am very materialistic, as well.

Just the other day, as I scanned the newspaper ads, I saw a sprawling mansion for sale and a Mercedes 400 E.

"I want those," I thought.

I have no way of getting them, but never let it be said that I'm an aesthete. Rabelais would be more of my kind of person.

California is a huge state, as everyone knows (but who ever said that a novel couldn't contain common knowledge?)

For the purpose of making this a superb, non-perturbing -- "perb" amd "terb" rhyme -- novel, the locale will be somewhat narrowed.

"Somewhat" is one of my favorite words. "Somewhat" is a monkey-wrench type word. For example: "Do you love me?" "Somewhat."

The narrowed locale will be, for the present, the sleepy little city of Los Angeles.

As you may have noticed, "Dear Reader," (one of my favorite condescentions from Jane Austen) these chapters are moving right along.

Why?

Because I am a mere robot writing the novel that's already written in my ever-diminishing mind?

That I am in a hurry because of an impending earthquake?

Well... no! It's my novel and I can have as many chapters in it as I want to! I don't even have to have chapters if I don't want to. I'm just being nice and giving you a few structural guidelines so don't push it! As you know, I could give up all semblance of standard practice, diss the punctuation rules and all of that, call it Modern and let you figure it out in some lonely graduate library cubicle.

So, be nice to me and I will write you a nice novel.

I will not make it too hard on your mind. After all, I am a nice person, comparatively speaking. Punctuation (etc.) is just politeness.

If you had been through everything I've been through, you might be dead.

So consider this a gift. I have every reason never to communicate with anyone again.

But, hey. What Fun would that be?

Oh nevermind: "fun" is one of those bugaboo words too. If you'd read T.S. Eliot's "Tradition and the Individual Talent" you'd know that.

But, be that as it may (and other such forgiving expressions) I will continue to communicate with you in this novel.

I don't care much for talking, as I always end up saying things I don't mean.

So read this. It's our best bet, as they say at the racetrack.

From me to you. With Love.

CHAPTER 4

The Op-ed Page of the L.A. Times

It often occurs to me that I am going crazy, but, I'm not. It was Moses Herzog, in Bellow's <u>Herzog</u>, who had that same thought but he added-- craziness was okay with him. And Vargas Llosa, in <u>Conversation in the Cathedral</u>, declared his undying love for nuts.

So, I am not going crazy and that makes me happy.

I have gathered together all the terms that are offensive to the mentally ill minority, however. I thought that perhaps one day I might write an article on their behalf and send it to the Op-ed page of the L.A. Times.

I have finished writing for the day.

Whether my life is in a shambles or ("whether it is"-- could be added there, but purely optional) not, I have finished writing for the day. "Northern Exposure" is on TV tonight.

I have been writing for one and a half hours, approximately.

It is time to eat dinner now. I guess I'll have a frozen burrito. They're pretty good... when they're unfrozen, that is.

If people don't quit pressuring me, I just might do something drastic. What does that mean-- "drastic?"

Join the Moonies? (Remember them?) I wonder whatever happened to all those people who got married all at once. Did they all get divorced together?

It is hard for me to live because of my love for words.

Los Angeles (duly narrowed, constricted)-- this chpt. begins on that unlucky number (handwritten) 13... superstitions, why are all these positively fossillike ideas still in my brain? How could any number be lucky! It's idiotic-- is the city I consider home.

When I begin feeling like Spielberg's E.T., yearning for "H...O...M...E...," it is Los Angeles I mean. "H..O..M..E..": Los Angeles.

Everyone knows (common knowlege) what Los Angeles is so I don't need to report any of The Facts (whatever those really are.) No one seems to know what facts really are, but everyone has his opinion about what facts are.

See, this is a postmodern novel: to call attention to a word, I just capitalize the first letter of a word that would usually be "in caps," as they say in the biz.

To be more like Dreiser, to have a more formal approach to the narrative, I begin thus: --but I don't like Dreiser. So I begin again.

I am trying to look forward to things.

I am trying to be happy.

Los Angeles-- you see, I have to write to be happy and there's the rub, as they say. (I think that's what they say.)

Los Angeles-- I must always be working on one writing project or another else I become a ... bit unhappy.

Los Angeles--

Los Angeles,

The way it sounds: Los Angeles...

a dreamy sound, Los Angeles...

You see, I write out the chapter title. That shows my carefulness.

I do not look back over the preceeding chapters. It is important to just keep moving forward, keep progressing, keep improving.

CHAPTER TWELVE

*My Soul
Is Like a Flank Steak*

And now the serious work is to begin.

Here we are on page 26 already (handwritten.)

"And at such a tender age...what a pity..."

Those remarks are vaguely connected to the on-going narrative. That happens all the time-- sentences just cross my mind, people saying things, "Oh, what a pity" and all of that. I suppose such remarks are just residue from the unconscious of years gone by, something I've heard perhaps, phrases that were a part of a conversation in days gone by. Ah well, "the unconscious"-- what a can of worms that was!

"...And at such a tender age... what a pity..." to be on page 26 already!

But being on page 26 already is not a pity at all: it's an accomplishment.

As for "tender age"-- well, I am not at such a tender age any longer, and if the truth be known, which it will, I never was that tender anyhow. I would say my soul is not a filet mignon. It is more like a flank steak.

Must the serious work begin?

Must it ever begin?

I suppose by "tender" age, ordinary people (people who think and talk like most other people) mean "young?"

Well, yes, I admit it, I was young once.

My youth-- which, as near as I can figger it, ended at about age 35 (in a cataclysmic manner)-- was, more or less, one big ache. So I will spare you the details. I realize that 35 years is a rather prolonged, elongated youth. But I was always slow in everything I did.

So, that takes care of the first 35 years.

Ages 35-39 were no great shakes.

At 40 I more or less started over again and that is partly what this novel is about.

So now you know.

The narrator of the novel is about 40 years old.

I do not really know if I can carry this novel through in a coherent manner ("or not"-- I think the "or not" is grammatically optional? or superfluous?) but I will try my best.

Geez. Back off! I'm only human!

I must have some thinkingtime each day.

If this is a stupid chapter, my heartfelt apologies. I am trying my best. If you'd try to write a novel, you'd see how hard it is and you'd be a little more understanding about this whole thing.

In Los Angeles people go to bed when they are supposed to. Nine or Ten o'clock seems like a good bedtime to me. Why do people stay up so late? Aren't they tired? It's like everyone is trying to squeeze as many things as possible into a day, like those things won't be there tomorrow, like things are going away and can't be done tomorrow, like people are afraid they will wake up tomorrow and everything will be gone. It's like a Heinz ketchup existence -- trying to squeeze the tomato of their life into the one-day bottle.

People are always trying to get everything done in one day.

What are people afraid of? Do they think they are going to die in their sleep?

Why do people stay up so late? Nine or ten o'clock seems like a good bedtime to me.

People need to ask: what would really happen if this wasn't done today?

Nine or ten o'clock seems like a good bedtime to me.

CHAPTER 15?

We're All Just Wheat Toast in the Toaster of Life

Los Angeles.

"'It was quite obvious.'" So says Italo Svevo.

What to say to that?

-"Yes, it was, wasn't it, 'quite obvious' that is, I mean to say."

-"Obvious things are so stupid."

-"Yes, and well, more than stupid, they are uncaring."

-"'It was quite obvious.'" So said Italo Svevo.

-"Obvious misdeeds-- what of those?"

-"Uh..."

-"Obvious faithlessness--"

-"Uh, well..."

-"What of those?"

-"'It was quite obvious.'"

-"Yes, it was."

*   *   *

So this is the loneliest job in the world, they say. That really belongs on the title page, that's the title of the chapter?

I am feeling belittled today.

Handwriting analysis-- really! I must make some decisions, I must decide what to leave in and what to leave out of this novel. Handwriting analysis-- stupid!

I could use a new electric pencil sharpener.

I like those mechanical pencils but the one I was using ran out, got all used up, so I continue on like many people: dully.

I could switch to a pen, which doesn't make any of these "scritching" noises, but then there's no erasing.

So this is the loneliest job in the world.

It is a Tuesday today for some reason, not that it matters. It could be Thursday or Wednesday, it makes no difference what day it is.

Does it make any difference what time it is? No, not really.

My life is basically over. What I mean by that is that it will be just about the same every day, today, and for the rest of my life. So, it is not really that my life is over. It is that my life is complete. I think that's what I mean, or, close enough anyway.

I do try to pop out with my individuality every now and then: that's me, wheat toast.

Individuality keeps life interesting.

What are we really? Mere pieces of wheat toast popped out of the toaster of life.

That would be a better title for the chapter: The Toaster of Life.

Ah Well. Speaking of constricted views, I could go and buy some fish and let them swim around the fish bowl thinking it's the ocean.

Did I ever tell you about my conversations with the fish? No one ever believed that my fish could talk but he could. It happened to Gunther Grass too and he wrote about it in <u>The Flounder</u>.

Anyway, it was an interesting day.

As you may or may not know, fish are usually loquacious.

We talked about improving our vocabularies, both of us agreeing that that was worthwhile.

Well, come to think of it, we talked about so many things that I think my conversations with the fish deserve a chapter all their own.

I have to break here anyway and go and take my socially-acceptable shower.

I have had lots of interesting conversations. I'll tell you about them, if I get around to it.

Since I am a capricious writer, this was one of my most propitious days.

When I first saw him, he looked rather sepulchral so I asked him what was wrong.

"No one has bothered to name me," he said, his small fins drooping somewhat.

"Ah well, what can it matter!" I proclaimed, my heart bursting with pathos.

"Well, one needs an identity," he said.

"Yes, of course."

A few moments passed in silence.

"Let's improve our vocabulary," I ventured to say at last, thinking I had hit upon a worthwhile topic.

"Okay," he said, swimming up to the side of the bowl and looking at me intently. "Where to begin?"

From that moment on we were the best of friends.

*   *   *

"I'll give you a word and then you give me one," he said, playfully.

"Okay. You start."

"Triskelion" he said professorially.

*   *   *

We continued our vocabulary game for many months and came to understand a great many useful words ("paraph" anyone?)

When we tired of the vocabulary game we played another.

I despaired somewhat that we couldn't play regular games together like badmitton and so on but, all in all, he was an Eudemon and kept me company for many a sesquipedalian hour.

Chapter 17 or 18

or Chapter 8 Million, What Can It Possibly Matter Now?

mind at work!

I don't know what I will do today exactly or really.

("Exactly" is such an antilife word, so aseptic, like something out of <u>Brave New World</u>.)

That's good. Messy is good. Like life.

"I"-- I always try always to start with "I", to keep hold of my life, to keep hold of my identity even as everyone works against one's identity, trying always to make one feel that one's personal life is not important

All those people that can not ever really love anyone...

Incapable of love: That is a very real defect!

Or maybe it just that they do not love me?

They do not know what love is? What it is like to truly love someone...

<u>Confessions of Zeno</u>-- what is it like to truly love someone?

So-- what's to do today?

One meaningful term, Credibility. And another, Credentials. In other words, I think that a thing can be judged as right or wrong according to who says it. If a certain person says something, then one can be sure that it is wrong.

End of philosophy for today: Good questions: How would you know? What credentials do you have in that area that would make your opinion valid?

* * *

It is no use.

I am completely miserable.

There is nothing I really want to talk about.

I am waiting to die, really.

If this is how life is going to continue, I don't really want to live it.

My true feelings, those.

I am always forced to say things I don't want to say.

You understand. Every once in a while, I get tired of lesser lights. I'm tired of how they've messed up the world and how they've messed up me.

So for dinner on this occluded Wednesday? Noodles. 5 packs for 79¢. And beef flavored too! What a crummy life I have. I'm so distraught!

I am completely miserable.

I have absolutely nothing to lose! Etc.!

So now what.

So I'm miserable.

What to do about it.

Surprise!

They were all wrong.

Everyone was wrong.

And here I am in our apartment. I have named our apartment Little Auschwitz.

Los Angeles.

In Zeno-- in "The Story of My Marriage" chapter, I have finally met a man who says the right things. In matters of romance and love, Zeno always says the right things. Zeno says the things I have always longed to hear! He knows the things to say to a woman that makes a woman feel loved! ("I would give it all up for her," he says early on.) It makes me feel that I wish I had known Zeno. I don't know if what he says is true or not-- but in an important sense they are very true. His words are nourishments to a woman's soul: the words I have always longed to hear! He seems to be able to address a woman's doubts, fears and needs.

Maybe that is why I do not like to talk much to people and why I do not want them to talk to me: they say the wrong things.

Where is the person who would say to me the things I need to hear?

Los Angeles, pity me! The creative powers are tiring and death may be near.

Ah well, early to bed...

CHAPTER 23

An Oculist, and Other Memories

Some of my favorite things in life, that make me enjoy the world better, are videos, chocolate, cigarettes, coffee, sweet rolls and the L.A. Times barbequed spare ribs and tacos. Dr. Peppers. Coconut cream pie is good too. Lots of foods I like that, this year, I will get to eat. That will make me happier, getting to eat the foods I like. Also going out and about sometimes is good, the health food store, for example the video store, the candy store, etc.

The Ventura Broadway shopping center-- not its designanted name The BuenaVentura Shopping Center Maybe?-- is one place I have wiled away many happy hours.

There is a Fox movie theatre across the street (the center is on Mills Road.) The shopping center has The Broadway, a place of many memories!

There is a bookstore there, Walden's I think-- or Dalton? Waldens, I think. A Hawaiian store with clothes from Hawaii. An oculist. Scott's apparel.

(I am reminded of Korbs-- but that's on another street-- by The Wagon Wheel and the day-old Arrowheat Bakery.) A See's Candy. A Thrifty's drug store.

And a J.C. Penney's. And a cafeteria, name forgotten-- a Loop's? Probably not. A Woolworth's that I didn't go in much. Kaiser's health food bar where I ate Hercules Shakes (health food shake with a raw egg.) 1 J. Magnin, which I didn't buy in. (I remember the downtown shop, "The Great Eastern" and so many other memories.) My life was in Ventura for so many years. A little sandwich shop on

Telegraph Road. All these places have so many memories for me, and good memories too! Jack in the Box on Seaward. Oh, how I love the whole city!

CHAPTER 24

___The General in His Labyrinth,___
___(a few notes)___

Some of the pgs. are missing because I used them to write down, work out, what was bothering me at the time. Since I consider them personal notes, I don't leave them in the book.

Of the remaining notes, I do not consider so personal...

(1) I have read, at last count, 6 of G.M.'s works.
(2) "... local tyrants."; other thoughts of interest on pgs. 18, 19, 22, 29, 31, 32, 33, 34, 35, (34, "...the lush diction...")
(3) 47, 68, 69.

During the day, in the past, I watched a funny video about baseball. Some of the players balanced a baseball on the front part of their hats. One put a pillow under his jersey and, during a rain delay, ran around the bases like a pregnant woman. In Japan, a player climbed up on the homerun fence and caught a ball.

I also watched a video about The Harlem Globetrotters. It was narrated by Louis Gossett, Jr., who wore a nice, red carnation on his sportscoat. Some of the players were Curly (who was bald) Reece Tatum, Wilt Chamberlain (for a while, and who was really, really tall) and Meadowlark Lemon. One of their antics was the rear-end bump of the ball. Their elaborate, pregame, warm up circle was really classic and funny. The greatest dribbler ever was Marques Haynes. In the later years, there was a female Globetrotter, Lynette Woodard. She led the U.S. woman's basketball team to a gold medal (in 1984) at the Olympics. The Harlem Globetrotters were a very important team for many reasons. I really enjoyed watching the video of them.

It is 8 o'clock in the morning now, on a Friday. I am up kind of early but that's okay. I went to bed last night around ten o'clock. I cleaned up the apartment some yesterday and had these burrito-like things for dinner.

The sun is shining bright today. And that's good.

So, back to a functional apartment life. What does that mean--"functional?" It means, first of all, that each person's emotional, spiritual, physical, and intellectual needs are met. Every person has 4 kinds of needs.

Question one: are my emotional, spiritual, physical, and intellectual needs being met?

All my needs are being met so I'm okay.

*   *   *

I have a lot of books around here, and that's good. I like to read.

I also like to write. When I write things down, I understand them better. When things are placed in my own words, they make more sense to me. In a way, writing is always a kind of translating of real life: placing things in my own words.

"...Never once have I...": one of those thoughts that just occur. Where did that come from? Is it something I've heard in my past? Who's phrase was that? What time period? Is it an emotion? Just something I overheard somewhere in passing, in some ordinary, everyday place like a grocery store?

I think it was Duras who wrote something to that effect, about things overheard from a hallway. I would like to read more of Duras' work. She is a great writer. Right now I don't have any of her books around.

I read Rhys, though, and loved her: a shining Intelligence, very illumined: So, what to do besides read?

Question two: why don't people feel bad about lying? Because they want to do certain things? They don't care if they lie or who they lie to, just so long as they get to do what they want to do? I have known many liars.

*   *   *

"I"-- to usually start each day with "I"-- makes me happy and healthy.

I.

It is Friday night and I am all alone. It is a quarter to seven. Dinner time, I suppose. It's just me and my movies tonight, as last night...

It's colder today: Saturday.

Not much happenin' around here.

Finished a load of laundry.

*   *   *

I want to improve my life in a major way!

I watched lots of movies: <u>The Sterile Cuckoo</u>, <u>Jonathan Livingstone Seagull</u>, <u>Barefoot in the Park</u>, and <u>Kramer vs. Kramer</u>.

I guess watching a movie is something I could do every weekend-- and other days if I want.

But perhaps I have gone through all this before: What's for today?

I remember writing something in my journal called "Will you Remember me?" I am sure that I later used that writing as notes for a polished work; that is, the writing went through a Sea Change.

My life fell completely apart, and I had to put it back together.

Sometimes I can not bear the thought of my life passing in this way.

*   *   *

Certain Despair: No one to count on in times of trouble. No where to turn. No on to Turn to.

"When the going gets rough, I'm nowhere around."
"When the going gets rough, don't count on me." Those are
the mottos of
Who can I count on? Who can I turn to?
("When the going gets rough, don't call me!")
I have no one.
Everyone can count on me but I can't count on anyone.
Everyone dumps their troubles on me but I have no one
to turn to. Everyone can depend on me, but I can depend
on no one.

I have no one!
Despair!

I am there for everyone but no one is there for me!

Alone!

When things go wrong everyone says Tell someone else!

How do I deal with completely selfish people?
Completely selfish!

CHAPTER 27

I hurt and it doesn't matter to anyone who has claimed to love me

I don't have a job anymore.

I don't have anything to do anymore.

My loss of a career was devastating.

This loss of meaning in my life, this loss of purposefulness, really hurts me.

All that is left for me to do is to be the best wife and mother I can be, since those are the two things I am.

I am a wife.

I am a mother.

I am something atleast. Maybe I can make that important, meaningful and purposeful.

That is what I can do: work on being the best wife and mother I can be. I can try to make being a mother and being a wife important, meaningful, and purposeful.

Maybe those are not such meaningless things to be? I can work on being the best wife and mother I can be?

That is all I am now.

It doesn't seem to be much, really.

But maybe those are good things to be? Maybe I can try to be a good mother and wife.

Just being a wife and mother isn't very fulfilling to me. But maybe, if I work at it, and discipline my mind, I can feel purposefulness, meaningfulness and importance in being the best wife and mother I can be.

Maybe being the best wife and mother I can be will help me feel fulfilled. Maybe being the best wife and mother I can be can be purposeful and meaningful and important: "Mrs." and "Mom."

I can have a fulfilling life with "Mrs." and "Mom" as my job titles. Maybe that is the answer solution to this dilemma: to just start with what you have and be the best at it that you can be, instead of always searching around yourself as a malcontent. Just look at what you are, start from there, and be the best at it that you can be. Improve on what you have. Don't throw out the old in the restless search for the new (as in <u>Brave New World</u>.)

To recognize what you are is important.

I am a wife and mother.

So, to revise that first thought: I don't have a job outside the apartment anymore.

Anyway... I do have a job. My job titles are "Wife" and "Mom."

The job descriptions for "Wife" "Mrs." and "Mom"...

That is the solution to that feeling of despair. To be happy with what I've got. To be happy with what I am. To start there, to build upon what I am and to be the best wife and mother I can be. Wife and mother, "Mrs." and "mom."

Those are my jobs.

That is what I am.

Wife and Mother.

It is a wrong idea that that is not enough to be.

"Mrs." and "Mom" are very important jobs.

I must suffuse some meaning into those jobs. They have taken a beating in years passed. They have been browbeaten.

It is enough to be.

"Mrs." and "Mom" are very important jobs.

"Mrs." and "Mom."

Yes, I do have a job.

Yes, I do have a job.

Yes, I do have a job.

I will be the best wife and mother I can be. I will start with what I have. I will start with who I am.

What does a wife do?

What does a mom do?

I have important jobs. I am and wife and mother.

So, Congratulations to me today.

The End

FUTURA

This is 1 (one) unless you want to designate things differently. Please feel free to redesignate this?

Let's look closer at a character sitting in a comfortable chair sipping coffee.

How did she get there? For instance. What about her background?
Her personal history? Should we just skip that?
Yes, I am inclined to skip that part.
What then?
Well let me think for a minute, geez.

Pause.

Thinking.

Still thinking.

Okay. I have it.

Futura got up from her chair and gingerly paced, walked through the kitchen to the sliding glass doors and opened them. It was a beautiful morninng in the neighborhood.

And besides, she could hear the ocean. The scent of ocean air hurried in.

On a personal note, that is, a note about the character's mind, which to my mind, is the most interesting thing about characters (but more on that later, possibly filed under writing theory) Futura hated to hurry. Or should I put that is the present tense, Futura hates to hurry. In any and every case you, dear reader, get the idea.

I will just rewrite that then, since I love my character. The ocean air does not hurry in. The ocean air casually strolls in. There. That's better.

Futura returned to her comfortable chair and finished her coffee.

You see why things get so difficult, to get the story up and going. In this day and age. Maybe it wasn't always like this.

It's hard to get anything done what with all these different elements. I have likened writing to that circus person that spins plates. Another image of writing I like is the salmon

Swimming upstream, although that also seems apt for life in general. Also the writer-as-punch ball. Or, at times, even doormat. That seems like a good name for a character, doormat. I like names that explain what people are. I think they used to name people that way in the old days, patience, charity, and could be an interesting, that is, a way of passing the time, practice, in this day and age. Internet savvy. Pitchers' agent. Cynicism everywhere. No more time. What happened to nature? Or, if I feel like trying a little harder... what are modern day virtues? Are they the same ones as two thousand years ago? But, since I prefer Kant to Aristotle, more on that later, I think I'll just leave it at that, that is, the paragraph ends here.

If you would like to redesignate paragraphs, feel free to do so.

Does this sentence go here or earlier or later or not at all or...?

I think ellipsis are pretty good. I don't have a lot against them, but more on that later. Filed possibly under writing theory.

So far all that my character has done is sit in a comfortable chair, sip coffee and open ???.

And now on to what she was thinking, which was...uh..

Looking ahead to my few weeks, let's see, on Thursday I give a talk at LACMA, Friday is the ceremony and my acceptance of the million dollar essay contest check, Monday after that is the Kafka transformational workshop, then later in the afternoon rehearsal for the traveling theatre company, just a bit part really but exciting, and then on Tuesday is uh salt water symposium, followed by a question and answer from the audience, if there is one, on the afternoon of the following Thursday is, let's see, can't be that many more planned yet, uh, oh yes the uh building fires near the pier safety committee meeting.

Futura rinsed out her coffee mug, placed it in the dishwasher, packed a breakfast-to-go, gathered her beach things and headed out walking down her street to the beach...

When last we saw Futura, she was headed on foot for the beach. And now, here she is. Peaceably passing away the hours, lolling away the hours I think is the idiom, maybe not, passing the time, on the beach. But what kind of story would this be if nothing happened? Well, that's fine with me, and many other writers. (that symbol for More On That Later, possibly filed under writing theory, from a awhile ago, goes here but I made the symbol so complicated that I can't remember what it is. I can be so stupid sometimes! I guess that if a person is going to use a symbol, she should chose a simple-minded one, or, to be nicer, a symbol easier to remember, otherwise, as Hurstwood gasped out in his last breaths, what's the use?)

As is readily, as is obvious, evident, Futura has her life plans ready to go for a few weeks, however, what about today?

Place for doodles, notes and other things

Quiz

Please spend some time, no more than 24 hours, trying to think about what moral behavior is. If you can, make a list of 20. If not, do your best which is, in itself, a kind of moral idea.

Tear along dotted line

From Futura's Journal

I wonder what it would be like to be really beautiful, I mean by the way that life is now, just as men see things, very beautiful, that kind of life, that kind of woman, I wonder what that would be like, like everywhere she goes everyone notices that she's very beautiful and maybe they wonder, what is she doing here? Shouldn't she be someplace great like the French Riviera or something? Or in the movies? It seems that a really beautiful person couldn't go just anywhere or be just anywhere, of course she would have to know that she is very beautiful, otherwise things could happen to her and she wouldn't know why or people would try to take advantage of her, yes she must know that she is beautiful

I was trying to think about the things that I really enjoy, to try to think about them and then I could have more fun and I started thinking about it and after awhile I understood that I never really had the privilege of even thinking about it and I began thinking about it, slowly at first and then I thought of one or two things that I like, that I really like and not the things that people tell me or the things that I am supposed to like for some reason and all that and I have always been in awe of those kind of people that know early and soon that they want and like and prefer this and that, how can they know that, it must be that their lives are better than mine, however I lately thought about and began thinking of the things that I really like

I try not to be sad because, not because it's a sin, I think some people and religions say that, and that could be right, however, I am not sad, I try not to be sad because of that reason and also because it is one of those things that can usually be remedied somehow and sometimes it doesn't take that much to remedy it, sometimes I don't know why I'm sad and that's okay, I try to remedy it though somehow and not to go on and on

It's strange to me that things that people remember and when I talk to people sometimes I never know the things they want to know, I guess it's that they measure and think about life differently than me or something because I end up being real dumb and not knowing what to say because I don't know the answer and I guess everyone remembers different things than me and that makes me wonder about the time before the things became memories, I mean when I am with people they are probably living it differently than me and therefore the memories are different

The End

Printed in the United States
By Bookmasters